THE ALPHA'S PROMISE

A DARK PARANORMAL ROMANCE

ALPHA DOMS

RENEE ROSE

RENEE ROSE ROMANCE

WANT FREE RENEE ROSE BOOKS?

Go to http://subscribepage.com/alphastemp to sign up for Renee Rose's newsletter and receive a free copy of *Alpha's Tempta-*

tion, Theirs to Protect, Owned by the Marine and more. In addition to the free stories, you will also get bonus epilogues, special pricing, exclusive previews and news of new releases.

Dearest reader,

When the publishing rights to the *Alpha Doms* series returned to me from Stormy Night Publications, the original publisher, I considered a major re-edit / re-write, as I'd done with my *Made Men* series. It's been nearly ten years since *The Alpha's Hunger* was published, and my writing ability, style, and content have evolved significantly. I still love kink, but I've moved away from the punishy-style, keeping it more in the sexy realm.

In the end, I decided to leave the series as is—a picture in time. Humbling though it may be to me, by leaving it as is, you can see my evolution as a storyteller. *The Alpha's Hunger* (2015) is my billionaire boss wolf shifter 1.0., *Alpha's Temptation* (2017) became 2.0 and *Big Bad Boss* (2024) is 3.0. Who knows what shape 4.0 will take?

As always, I am eternally grateful to you, the reader, who keeps me writing, pushing my craft, and learning to find new depth with each story I tell. Thank you for your readership now, and if you've been with me since the beginning, a million kisses for sticking with me all this time.

ACKNOWLEDGMENTS

A huge thank you to Whitney Cartwright for the inside scoop on the Colorado Springs real estate market, including videos of homes in the Old North neighborhood!

Just a few more weeks and I'm out of here.

Melissa headed up the sidewalk to the rundown rental house where she and her loser, soon to be ex-boyfriend had lived for the past eight months. She couldn't wait to be done with the place. Her heels clicked on the concrete, pencil skirt too constraining in the early June heat after a long day showing houses.

She braced herself for the annoying clutter of half-filled moving boxes. At least it meant that in less than a month Jeremy would be out of her life, forever.

The relationship never should've happened in the first place. She'd mistaken bonding in a crisis situation—Jeremy had saved her life after he and his buddy had kidnapped her last year—for true love.

Maybe she'd just wanted what her sister had with her new husband.

In another of her classic bad judgement moves, she'd forgiven him for the kidnapping, been grateful for his change of heart. Moved in with the guy who'd put her life in danger. That f-ed up statement pretty much summed everything up. She was too loyal, too trusting. Thought that the attraction would last. It hadn't. Four months later she'd been totally over him, but it had taken her four more to figure out how to get out of their lease, even after they'd broken up. Her stuff was already packed into boxes. By this time next month she'd be free of Jeremy and this dump.

She unlocked the door and pushed it open, then stopped dead with a gasp.

The place had been wrecked. Destroyed.

Boxes had been opened and emptied—stuff was strewn everywhere. The pottery dishes she'd bought from her artist friend in college lay in a broken heap, paintings had been torn from the walls and smashed.

A sob rose in her throat. She turned in a slow circle, her heart thumping hard in her chest. When she saw the maroon spray-painted words scrawled across the back wall, she screamed.

Pay up by Friday or you both die.

A sheet of ice flashed through her. She literally couldn't move, couldn't breathe. Her body trembled all over. Her hand closed around her cell phone, but something stopped her from calling 911.

This wasn't just a break-in. It was personal. And it had something to do with Jeremy. Had something happened at the dispensary? He was always afraid they'd be robbed at gunpoint—it had happened at other dispensaries because they took in a large amount of cash.

Oh, God. She should've known. She should've run fast and hard from Jeremy the moment they were free of the kidnapping trauma.

He had a knack for landing in trouble. He associated with the wrong sorts of people. He liked to party and used drugs. He might even deal harder stuff out the back door of the dispensary—she didn't know, she'd been turning a blind eye to all that.

Would calling the cops ensure someone's death? She gulped. Hers?

With trembling fingers, she dialed her twin sister instead. Ashley and Ben had gone to the Canary Islands for their honeymoon. She shouldn't bother them, but… she really didn't know what else to do.

"Hey, Mel," her sister's voice called gaily through the earpiece.

"I'm sorry to bother you."

Her sister instantly picked up on the pinched, wobbly quality of her voice. "What is it, Mel? What happened?" Ashley asked sharply.

"I-I'm not sure. I just came home and the place has been wrecked. And there's a spray-painted message on the wall." She told her sister what it said, without having to voice her suspicions about it being some trouble of Jeremy's. Ben and Ashley already had the lowest opinion of him.

"I'm going to check upstairs, do you mind staying on the phone with me?"

"Of course I don't mind, but do you think you should call the police?"

She walked up the stairs, holding the phone tight against her ear, as if it somehow made her sister closer.

Ben's sharp tones had started at the mention of police, and she listened to her sister explain to him what had happened.

The intruders had trashed the bedroom upstairs, too. Her dresser drawers had been dumped onto the floor, hamper unloaded. It looked like they'd even torn the carpet up from the floor. What had they been looking for? Money?

"Mel? Ben's going to call someone he knows in Colorado Springs, so just sit tight, okay?"

"Okay." She was more relieved than she cared to admit to hear that Ben knew what to do.

"I'll call you right back," Ashley promised.

She hung up and stared at the mess, tears burning her eyes. What should she do? She wished she could pack up all her stuff and get out that second, but she didn't know where to go. Where could she rent a place on such short notice? And she didn't want to rent, dammit, she'd been so excited to buy her own place.

Ben Stone, her twin sister's wealthy new husband, had offered to help her with a down payment so she could buy a house of her own.

The sound of a car door slamming made her look out the window. Jeremy had better have a solution for—

But it wasn't Jeremy.

Three lethal-looking guys got out of a dark blue Range Rover and strode purposefully to the front door. They didn't bother knocking and she stupidly hadn't locked it.

Holy hell. They were here, *in the house*. They were going to kill her.

Heart jammed up high in her throat, she dived for the closet, squirrelling back behind the clothes.

Please don't let them search the house.

Her phone lit up, the first note of the ring sending her into a wild swiping frenzy to shut it off. It went silent. She held her breath, listening to hear if the men downstairs had noticed, but only heard the sound of their voices calling to each other. Were they moving in to wait for her and Jeremy?

Her hands shook so hard, she could hardly read the phone, but saw it had been Ashley calling.

She texted her back.

They're in the house.

~

CODY STEELE WASHED the plaster off his trowel and wiped everything clean. Almost finished—just a couple of quick coats of paint over this repaired hole in the wall and the house would be ready to go on the market. Buying historic buildings and homes, fixing them up and selling for a tidy profit had put his restless, hands-on personality to good use. CJ Steele properties had become well known in Colorado Springs for their real estate successes and his company provided jobs for most of the wolves in his pack.

Not bad, considering his dad had thrown him out of the pack at sixteen, saying he'd never amount to anything. It was a source of pride that he'd started and made his business successful completely on his own, starting a pack in a city where they'd previously been loose members of the Denver pack.

His cell phone buzzed and he pulled it out of his pocket and frowned. Ben Stone, the alpha from Denver. What in the hell did he want?

He answered it. "Cody speaking."

"Cody? Ben Stone, from Denver."

"I know who you are."

"I need a favor from you—a big one." There was a curt sense of urgency in the guy's voice.

He ground his molars. Pretty presumptuous for a guy who hadn't offered him or his pack even a hello since he took over as alpha nine months ago. "I don't recall owing you one."

Stone didn't hesitate. "I'll be the one owing. My sister-in-law lives in Colorado Springs and she's run into trouble. I'm out of the country or I'd come down myself to handle things."

"What kind of trouble?"

"Her place got broken into. There's a threatening message spray-painted on the wall. Probably her loser ex-boyfriend got himself into some trouble, but she's not involved. I need you to keep her safe."

Fuck.

This was the last thing he wanted to get involved in. But having Ben Stone in his debt would only be a good thing for his pack. Ben had all kinds of resources, money being at the top of the list. He also had a large pack with members of every skill set, and being friendly with them would mean he'd never have to turn to his father's pack for help. And he'd rather die than do that.

"Steele?"

He blew out his breath. "Yeah, okay. What's the address?"

"I'll text it to you. You'll go right now?"

"I'll go. What's her name?"

"Melissa. Steele—alpha's promise you'll give her pack protection."

Shit. What in the hell was he getting himself into? Stone wanted him to vow his own life to protect her. Well, that's what wolves did.

"Yeah," he grunted. "Alpha's promise."

"Thank you."

He closed his eyes and rubbed a hand across his face. He'd live to regret this.

Because his pickup was full of painting supplies, he left it in front of the house and jogged the few blocks to his own place, where he hopped on his motorcycle and checked the address Ben had texted.

His wolf instincts kicked into gear before he got there, putting him on high alert. He cut the engine and coasted silently up to a small two-story house. A dark blue Range Rover was parked in front, behind a white Toyota pickup. Tingles of warning raced across his skin.

The front door stood open and male voices barked inside.

He skirted the building to peer through a window. Three guys sat on the couch. They all sported guns and one wore a fancy suit.

A chill made the hairs on the back of his neck bristle. Looked like Junior Rabago, a drug dealer out of Denver. He moved heavier drugs like cocaine and heroin through one of the local marijuana dispensaries. If Ben's sister-in-law was tied to him, this was bigger trouble than he'd imagined.

Fuckity fuck fuck. He should not have offered an alpha's promise to Ben for this. Now protection had just turned into a rescue. And he didn't even have a gun on him.

Ben had said his sister-in-law was here now. Had they killed her already? Or had she managed to escape in time? He scented the air. He didn't smell blood. Only the fresh scent of humans— mostly male, maybe one female. No wolves. He looked up the building. A window stood open on the second floor.

Was he nuts for thinking about climbing up there? Probably. But he couldn't see what other choice he had. It was that or camp out here to wait for the guys to leave and they didn't look likely to leave any time soon. He gripped the rain spout, hoping it was strong enough to hold his weight. It creaked, the metal scraping the side of the brick building when he swung onto it, but it didn't pull away from the building. He scaled it to the roof, then crept to the area above the open window and lowered his body down over the side, his toes landing on the sill.

The screen came out easily and he tossed it down to the grass below. He crept into what appeared to be a bedroom, which had been completely trashed. The human female scent was stronger here—an alluring smell, despite the fact that it didn't come from a she-wolf.

His instincts blared. Someone was in the room. He trained his sensitive ears and heard breathing. A rapid heartbeat. It came from the closet. Melissa? No—the scent was decidedly human.

He walked over and eased the door open, trying not to make any noise to alert the guys downstairs. Female clothing packed the closet—dresses and suits hung from hangers, filling the entire space. He didn't see the woman, but the staccato beat of her heart and the metallic scent of fear drew his attention to the back corner.

With a swift movement, he yanked the clothing to the side and reached out to snatch her, clamping one hand over her mouth to keep her silent. He hadn't planned for her knee connecting with his groin.

He doubled over, only barely preventing a groan from leaving his mouth.

The young woman tried to shove past him, but he grabbed her from behind, wrapping one arm around her waist, covering her mouth with the other hand. The contact sent a jolt of something unfamiliar through him. Like a warning, only more pleasant. The hairs stood up on the back of his neck. "Melissa?"

Maybe it wasn't her. The human struggled with

more force than he'd expect out of a human female, her body lithe and strong beneath the soft exterior. Wrestling her aroused his inner beast, his cock thickening as if this were some wild mating dance, instead of a life or death situation.

"Ben Stone sent me," he growled low in her ear, in case she was the female he was supposed to save. Her apples and cinnamon scent filled his nostrils, exciting his body, despite the situation. Despite the fact that wolves aren't attracted to humans.

She went still.

Okaaay. Ben Stone's sister-in-law was human. Which meant Stone's wife must be, too. He hadn't heard that, although Stone's pack would probably not be in a hurry to spread that information.

She twisted to look back at him, eyes wide with fear. Her beauty struck him like another jab to the balls. Her eyes were wide and blue, thick glossy hair hung in long reddish-brown waves. He'd never seen such a beautiful human in his life. He eased the hand from her mouth to reveal lush lips, trembling with fear.

"I'm the rescue wagon," he said sardonically. It sounded more bitter than he felt, only because his attraction to her had taken him by surprise and he didn't like surprises.

Her lips parted but she didn't speak.

He didn't have a weapon and those guys down there had guns. Which meant fighting their way out was a no-go, especially since she was a weak human. "We'll have to go out the window. I'll jump down and catch you when you follow."

Her big blue eyes bugged out. "We can't. This is a second story," she whispered.

He turned her around to face him. "Do you know what I am?"

Please say she at least knew that her brother-in-law was a shifter.

She gave him an up and down sweep, gaze traveling over the paint-splattered clothes, the tattoos on his arms, his unshaven face. He realized his appearance was in sharp contrast to hers—she wore a tight pencil skirt and silk blouse, like some kind of young professional. Was her lip curling with distaste?

He was well familiar with condescension, the scorn for an uneducated manual laborer who looked more like a criminal than Colorado Springs' top real estate investor. For some reason, it bothered him this time, when usually he didn't give two fucks what people thought of him or his tough-guy appearance.

She swallowed, then licked her lips. "Wolf?"

He nodded, taking her hand and tugging her toward the window. "That's right, princess. Your wolf in shining armor. You jump, I'll catch."

Doubt scrambled her features. She glanced over her shoulder at the door, perhaps wondering if there was another way out. Her skin appeared ashen, but she nodded.

He jumped out the window, landing in a crouch on the grass below. When he turned to look for her, though, she stood frozen, looking down.

Shit. *Come on.* He wanted to yell up, but of course couldn't risk making a sound. A sense of urgency washed over him, his instincts roaring danger, his need to protect a pack mate—even a new foster mate like her—kicking into high gear. No, his need went beyond pack mate. It had something to do with those big beautiful eyes and her delectable scent, but he couldn't to dissect that now.

He gestured urgently.

Still, she remained, looking again to the door, then down at him.

Hell, if one of the assholes from downstairs walked in there, he'd have no way to protect her now—he wouldn't be able to climb back up quickly enough. And he'd made a sacred oath to keep her safe.

Her head whipped back from looking over the door, eyes wild. Someone must be approaching. She squatted on the window's edge.

He made a frantic motion for her to jump. She twisted toward the door again and gave a scream, then launched herself into the air.

A male shout cracked the air as she plummeted toward him, but he didn't dare take his eyes from her falling body to see who had arrived. She dropped into his arms and he staggered at the impact, but then took off running, as fast as he could.

More shouting.

He made it to his bike and dropped her on the back of it, wishing he had a helmet for her fragile human skull. She looked horrified, her pencil skirt forced all the way up so she could straddle the seat, revealing creamy white thighs and pink lace panties.

Too bad, princess.

He hit the ignition button and the motorcycle spluttered. Dammit.

Two men ran out of the front door, waving guns.

The bike roared to life. He hit the gas and the back wheel skidded out behind them as they charged away.

2

———

Melissa screamed and wrapped her arms around her tattooed rescuer's waist as the motorcycle nearly popped a wheelie tearing down the back alleyway. He grasped her arm, as if to make sure she wouldn't let go.

"I'll hang on, you put both hands on the handlebars," she shouted, squinting her eyes as the blur of trees and houses whipped past.

His abs were hard as rock under her fists. In fact, she was pretty sure his entire body strained with solid muscle. He looked like he worked hard with his hands. The worn work jeans and stained t-shirt were sexy in that rough and scruffy kind of look that was *way* too much her thing.

But she needed to get away from the 'bad boy' attraction. It had only landed her in trouble.

She twisted to look behind them and caught a

glimpse of the blue car that had brought the mafia assholes to her apartment. "They're onto us," she yelled.

Her rescuer hit the gas again and they screeched around a corner, skidding out. He slipped between two buildings, around a corner. She couldn't keep track of where they were going—the dumpsters and buildings flashed by too fast. She had to squeeze her eyes shut against the wind.

In another moment, he screeched up a driveway and leaned the bike all the way to the side, skidding under a garage door halfway in flight. In a flash, he dismounted from the bike and yanked her off. The garage door had already reversed directions to come down, shutting them in.

She wobbled on her heels and tugged her skirt down over her ass. Her heart rapped against her ribs in a painful rhythm. They were in a huge garage. More of a workshop, actually, with saws and a workbench. Shelves lined every wall, stacked with paint, solvents, tools, supplies of every kind. Was this his workplace?

Her rescuer stalked toward her. Everything about him screamed scary tough—the bulging muscles of his arms, the tattoos that sprawled from under his short sleeves and even decorated his knuckles, the five o'clock shadow on his sturdy, square jaw, the menacing snarl of his expression. Seriously—he didn't look any more trustworthy than Jeremy or the assholes who'd been waiting at their place for him. Had she been right to leave with him?

She wobbled on her heels. "Who are you?"

He passed her and jerked open a door. "Get inside."

Right. Not the time for introductions. She scooted past him, trying to ignore the size of his muscles as she brushed his hard body, or the way her body reacted to his nearness. A flush of heat washed over her, warming up her icy fingers and face, thawing a fraction of the fear that nearly over-whelmed her back in that closet.

Of course she tripped, her heel catching the carpet as she passed him. He caught her elbow to stabilize her and she fell against his chest.

Wow.

He had slate gray eyes that were striking against his tanned skin and sun-bleached hair. As they stared at each other, his nostrils flared. The gray irises flickered to pale ice blue.

She gasped.

He shoved her away from him and blinked, averting his head. She wondered why he tried to hide his wolf—he'd already acknowledged what he was.

"What color are you?" she blurted. "I mean, when you shift?" It was a stupid question to ask. She ought to start with his name or how he knew

Ben, but the glimpse of those lupine eyes had her curious.

He twisted back to look at her. The irises had returned to gray.

"Silver."

A ripple of something went through her body—excitement, maybe. She suddenly desperately wanted to see him in wolf form. She knew he'd be incredible. Powerful and terrifying. Beautiful, even.

But no. She needed to stop this. Tamp down any attraction she had for the hot male who looked like trouble. She needed to start finding nice, upstanding men attractive. The kind without tattoos and worn-out jeans. The kind who wore ties to work and saved their money in tax-free retirement accounts.

She'd worked all year to get herself out of the party lifestyle. She'd taken the test to become a real estate agent and cut back her nights as a bartender. She'd been so close to getting rid of Jeremy and getting a real start. Now there were people trying to kill her because of him.

"You hurt?" The guttural voice sounded right behind her and she jumped and spun. Amusement flickered on his face.

She stuck out her hand, pulling out her best professional real estate agent persona, chin jutting high. "I'm Melissa, and you are—?"

His jaw tightened. Apparently, he didn't like

that. He ignored her hand and walked to the bookshelf in the small, dimly lit room. "Cody," he said gruffly. He shoved aside some books and withdrew a gun, which he tucked in the waistband at the back of his jeans.

She probably should have started with *thank you* instead of calling him on his manners, but now that he'd snubbed her, her spine had gone even straighter. She looked around the dank man cave and sniffed. "Is this your place?"

His eyes narrowed. "Sorry it's not the Taj Mahal, princess. I didn't know I'd be hosting Ben Stone's hoity-toity *human* sister-in-law." He sneered the word *human* like it disgusted him.

She bristled. Did he think because Ben was rich, she was too? "I appreciate the rescue, but you don't need to entertain me. If I could just borrow your phone—" She'd dropped hers in the closet when he'd grabbed her. She needed to warn Jeremy about those guys before he got killed. She may not love the guy, but she owed him her life.

He already had his phone out and up to his ear. "Yeah, I got her."

She heard the intonations of a male voice on the other end. Was it Ben? A slice of fear ripped through her. What if this guy hadn't been sent by Ben? Maybe it was another enemy of Ben's, like the South American pack that had tried to kill her twin Ashley last year? He hadn't told her anything other than that Ben Stone had sent him. And he sure as hell looked like trouble.

She inched toward the door.

"You didn't tell me how bad her trouble is." He paused as Ben said something. "Yeah, Junior Rabago and his guys... you know—the mobster. They were camped out at her place. They own one of the local dispensaries—push heavier drugs through it. I found her hiding in the closet and got her out of there, but they saw us leaving. Don't think they can trace us, because we lost them and the plates on my bike aren't good... Yeah, I'm ready for them, if they come." He peered out the blinds without moving them.

It wasn't a good sign that the plates on his bike weren't good. Definitely another lowlife. She leaned her back against the door. She wanted to hear this conversation, in case it was with Ben, but also needed to be ready to run.

Cody glanced over and narrowed his eyes, as if he knew exactly what she was doing. "You didn't mention she was human." Again, he said it like she was a stinky piece of dog poo that he'd gotten on his shoe. He stalked toward her with an expression of dark intent.

This time she heard the response from the other speaker on the phone loud and clear. *"You got a problem with that?"* That definitely sounded like Ben.

"No." Cody threw a hand out next to her head

to lean against the door, caging her with his body. Awareness lit up her skin, a wash of prickles heating everywhere he came close to touching her. "Where do you think you're going?" he growled.

"Hey. You'd better treat her right," came Ben's bark from the other end. Her brother-in-law was as gruff as this guy—he just seemed more refined because he wore a suit and owned a half billion dollar company.

Cody lowered his face, almost leaning his forehead against hers, eye to eye. She had a feeling it was a wolf thing. He probably wanted her to drop her gaze and submit, but the challenge only made her grit her teeth and stare back with more daring.

"If I'm going to keep her safe, she's going to have to follow orders."

"Mistreat her and there will be hell to pay," Ben gritted. "Put her on the phone."

Cody flicked his brows and held his phone to her ear. She snatched it away from him and ducked under his arm, stalking away with the haughtiest pride she could muster, which of course, was ruined when she tripped again on her damn high heel. Fucking shoes! She kicked them off.

"Hi, Ben," she said breathlessly.

"Melissa. Are you hurt?"

"I'm okay. Just… scared."

"Who were those guys, do you know?"

"No. Jeremy and I weren't really talking since

we broke up. We just sort of cohabitated out of necessity."

"Dammit, Melissa, I said I would help you buy a house."

"I know, I know. I've been looking. I was already half packed to move out."

"Listen, Ashley and I will fly back early and—"

"No," she interrupted. "Do *not* cut your honeymoon short for this. I'm fine. Cody got me out of there." She flicked a glance at her hot rescuer. "You don't need to come."

She already hated herself for needing—once again—to be rescued by her sister, whose life was always together, who always did the right thing. If Ashley and Ben came home early on account of her, she would be the asshole who ruined their honeymoon for the rest of their lives.

Cody peeked through the closed blinds again. He looked so damn alert and capable, like a bad-ass Navy SEAL, or Special Ops agent. If he was truly on her side, she'd be safe.

Ben cursed. "You need to stick with Cody. Do everything he tells you. He's alpha there, do you know what that means?"

"Not exactly."

Ben blew out his breath. She heard her sister say something in the background and then her voice came on.

"Am I on speaker?" she asked in a low voice.

"No." Melissa walked to the far side of the room, facing away from Cody, as if that would prevent him from hearing her conversation.

"Hey, wolves are all about the pack order, you know. So he's going to be overbearing and dominant. He's the boss, if you know what I mean. Just try not to let it get to you."

She snorted, looking over at Cody, who had crossed his arms over his massive chest, watching her with those assessing gray eyes.

Yep. Overbearing and dominant.

Her pussy clenched again. But that wasn't right. It was Ashley who was into the authority figure type, not her. She just did bad boys. Or used to. Now she was doing suits and ties. Business owners or CPAs. Or maybe a nice lawyer. A dentist, even.

She couldn't stop herself from looking over at Cody again. Her pussy felt hot and wet under her skirt. An image of that well-built, tattooed man pushing her over the seat of his motorcycle and spanking her ass flashed before her mind and she flushed and turned away.

His nostrils flared and he shot her a surprised look. The edges of his lips curled.

Holy hell. Did he read minds?

Ben returned to the line. "Melissa? Give the phone back to Cody." He was a man of few words, her brother-in-law. No *please* or *take care.*

But he did take care of her, she had to admit.

His offer to buy her a house had thrilled her. She wasn't going to let him buy the house outright. Just help her with a down payment. She'd get a house she could afford once he got her started. She knew just what she wanted—a CJ Steele house. One of the lovingly restored houses in Colorado Springs' oldest neighborhoods. She adored the CJ Steele company's work and admired the hell out of Steele, the up and coming real estate mogul who had made a small fortune buying and flipping houses over the past eight years. Her dream was to be his agent.

She handed the phone back to Cody and listened to another terse exchange before he hung up.

He sent a speculative gaze in her direction. "You'll stay here until it all blows over."

Only because he already had her off-balance and she didn't want him to have the upper hand, she curled her lip and looked around as if the place wasn't up to her standards. As if she hadn't already been living with Jeremy, the slob of the year. The place wasn't bad, but it could use a good cleaning. And it was a typical man cave. Small, basic, everything in dark colors like hunter green and navy blue.

His brows slammed down and he stalked past her. "I'm sorry it doesn't suit you, princess. Next time I'll make sure to rent a mansion for your sleepover."

The word *sleepover* sparked a nervous flutter in her belly as it became real that she'd actually be sleeping here with this meathead. She glanced toward the bedroom. There was only one, as far as she could see. His place had used all the square footage on the workshop/garage—at least fifteen hundred square feet. The inside was just a combination kitchen/living room, and a small bedroom and bathroom, as far as she could tell. Another eight hundred square feet. And yes, the realtor in her had assessed the property and its approximate market value—about one hundred and fifty grand —the moment she'd walked in.

"May I use your phone? I have to warn Jeremy."

His eyes narrowed. "Your boyfriend?"

"Ex."

"Don't you think he already knows? I'm guessing you weren't the one who got on the wrong side of Junior Rabago."

She pursed her lips and held out her hand. "Please? I don't want him to come home and get shot, okay?"

Cody's fingers flexed into a fist before they reopened and dug his phone from his pocket. "What are you doing with a guy like that, anyway?"

She frowned. Who was he to judge her taste in men? Especially when he didn't look like the kind of guy you'd bring home to Mother, either? The fact that he was right irritated her even more. "Your phone?"

He scowled and dropped it in her palm.

She dialed Jeremy's number, but he didn't pick up. Of course he might be afraid to answer a number he didn't recognize. She hit end and texted him.

Don't go home. Mafia-looking guys at our house. ~Melissa

He didn't answer. Was he already dead? What was the money they wanted paid by Friday?

Reluctantly, she handed the phone back and looked around the small living quarters again. How long would she be here?

"I need to get my purse and clothes at some point. Do you think those guys are gone from my place?"

Cody frowned. "There's no way in hell you're going near your place, not until I know it's safe. I can pick you up a few things at Walmart or something."

"Walmart?" She actually had no beef with Walmart, but he'd pegged her as a princess, so she was playing the part.

A tic in his jaw signaled his irritation. He stepped toward her, and she took a step back, half thrilled, half worried she'd bitten off more than she could chew. He gripped her upper arms. There was domination and authority in the way he held her, but his touch wasn't rough. In fact, the heat of his large, work-roughened palms on her skin sent flames of desire licking through her.

"Baby, you'll wear what I get you, or you can trot around in your panties for all I care." He leaned closer to her ear. "Actually, I *would* prefer the latter."

She worked to swallow, heat suffusing her core. Whether it was from his touch or the suggestion of strutting around half naked in front of him, she wasn't sure.

Cody inhaled and caught a whiff of Melissa's arousal. In a flash, his vision domed, the beast within him roaring to the surface.

What the fuck?

He blinked and released her, stepping back, away from her sexy little body. Yeah, she was hot—all soft curves and smooth skin with a beautiful face to match, but her personality left something to be desired. She was clearly stuck-up. And *human*. That ought to be enough of a turn-off right there, not that he minded sex with a human female now and then. It's just that his taste—whether in she-wolf or human female—ran more toward tougher women. The kind who liked it rough and understood the rules—that he didn't commit or make any promises. The sex was gratuitous, for their mutual pleasure, no strings attached.

"I can't wear cheap, ill-fitting clothes to show houses."

Real estate agent. It figured. He should've pegged her profession from the start. He had enough experience with agents. Bloodthirsty sharks, all of them.

"You won't be showing houses. When I said you're staying here, I meant *inside this house at all times*. If you think Junior Rabago won't wait for you at work, honey, you're not as smart as you look."

Consternation puckered her beautiful face. "Cody, I have houses to show. I won't go to the office, but—"

"*No.*" He made his voice as hard and forbidding as he knew how, not that the girl seemed to respond to his alpha dominance in any way. Which was another source of irritation. For the fortieth time, he kicked himself for making a promise to Ben Stone.

But no. Even as he imagined walking away from her little drama, he knew, promise or not, he'd protect this woman with his life, even as maddening as he found her. She didn't deserve whatever kind of trouble was falling down around her ears. Besides, there was something magnetic between them—some chemistry that was highly unusual between a shifter and a human. He was dying to explore it.

She lifted her chin, her big blue eyes challenging him. "How are you going to stop me?" She sounded a little breathless, which sent a kick of lust straight to his cock. He caught a whiff of her arousal again and was suddenly sure she had an inkling how he'd stop her, and wanted a taste of it. Maybe there was *one way* she responded to alpha dominance. The best way, in his opinion.

"I'm thinking, maybe something like this." He brought his hands to her waist and turned her, then picked up her small, smooth hands and placed them on the wall, one at a time. Like before, just touching her bare skin fired his inner wolf. He stroked his palms up her arms to her shoulders, savoring her soft skin. He slid them down her sides until he reached her hips, then he lifted one hand and brought it sharply down on her ass.

Her sharp intake of breath made his cock throb. "I think your sister warned you about me," he rumbled in her ear, his voice deeper and more gravelly than usual.

The silly girl didn't know wolves have excellent hearing. Walking to the other side of a room didn't preclude him from hearing every word of their conversation.

She didn't answer, but appeared to be frozen, listening intently, waiting. He caught no sign that he'd intimidated her. No, all he got was interest. That's what he'd smelled when she was on the phone, too. Good, that was the way he wanted it. He'd feel like a douchebag if he genuinely scared her.

"If you try to leave here, I'll spank you until this perfect ass is pink and your sweet little pussy is dripping wet."

Pink stained her cheeks. Her exhale sounded shaky. She didn't look at him, but remained in the position he'd put her, staring at the wall. The heady scent of her arousal told him he'd already achieved the second goal. And damn, he'd never wanted a human this badly before.

"Let me know if you want me to take care of that ache between your legs," he murmured, then stepped back. His voice sounded rough and deep. "I'd be happy to fuck the princess right out of you."

He shouldn't have said it. Not when he'd just gotten her to warm to him.

She drew herself up, yanking her hands away from the wall and spinning on him, cheeks flushed red. "Nice. Real nice." She lifted her chin and marched right for the front door.

"Don't do it," he warned.

She took a final look over her shoulder at him and threw the door wide, taking off running the minute she stepped outside.

His inner wolf took over. Before he could rein

himself in, he charged after her, vision domed, the thrill of the hunt upon him. No, the thrill of mating. In a flash, he was upon her, the animal in him roaring to…

Could it be?

Mark.

His inner wolf wanted to mate with her—permanently.

He caught her and carried her back into the house. Her scent filled his nostrils, making it impossible for him to regain control. His body wouldn't obey the command from his brain to put her down. She was his she-wolf and he needed to claim her, to make her his, to embed his scent in her, forever. With one arm wrapped around her waist, his free hand went under her skirt straight to her core. His lips went to her neck. Without any permission from his brain, his fingers rubbed her clit over her lacy panties.

"Cody!" she choked on his name and the shock in her voice brought his senses back.

"Fuck." He released her like she was on fire and backed away. "Christ, I'm sorry."

She whirled, her eyes widening at what she saw. His irises had to be ice blue, showing his wolf. Fuck, were his teeth out, too?

That didn't make sense. Why would he want to mark a human?

He shook his head, trying to recover his human self, his rational mind.

He held his palms up in surrender. "I didn't mean to lose control. That was… unexpected."

As his vision returned to normal, he scrubbed a hand over his face and drew several deep, cleansing breaths. Melissa's cheeks were flushed, her erect nipples showing through her bra and blouse.

He couldn't think what to say, except the first thing that popped into his head. "You nearly got fucked within an inch of your life."

She let out a shaky exhale.

He touched his teeth with the tip of his tongue. They felt normal now, but he knew he'd been about to mark her. The sweet secretion he would've embedded in her skin pooled in his mouth.

He glared at her, as if it were all her fault. "Never run from an aroused wolf. Especially not an alpha. It triggers the instinct to claim."

She blinked.

Way to blame the victim, asshole.

Fucking hell. He'd screwed this situation up royally.

You're a sorry excuse for a wolf. You'll never amount to anything. The only female who would ever lower herself to mate you is a human. His father's sneering prediction the night he'd tossed him out on his ass at age sixteen came ringing back in his ears.

He stabbed his fingers through his hair. Not

even a human woman would have an asshole like him. Despite all these years of trying to prove he could make it his own way, he was still as bad as that wild teenage wolf his father hadn't seen fit to keep in his pack.

"I'm sorry, Melissa. I didn't mean to force myself on you. Are you okay?"

Her head wobbled around on her neck, and she opened her lips, but no sound came out. He hated seeing her like that, wanted the uppity little real estate agent to return and insult him. But it was probably just as well she kept silent. If they went back to their verbal sparring, he wasn't sure he'd be able to hold back—she had his lust on a knife's edge as it was.

Even with his brain back in function, his cock strained painfully at his jeans.

He walked to his dresser and pulled out a t-shirt and pair of boxer briefs and tossed them near her on the bed. "You can wear these for now. I'll get you some clothes in the morning."

She didn't answer or move. Her breath pumped rapidly in her chest, berry lips parted.

"Are you hungry?"

He half expected her not to answer—he'd deserve the silent treatment after what he'd almost done, but she nodded immediately. He tried to think what he had in the house. Not much. He'd have to go grocery shopping for her too.

Taking care of anyone besides himself was an entirely foreign proposition. As alpha, he'd lay down his life for any of his pack mates, but that didn't mean he had to worry about their basic needs. They were all young and tough like him.

This little human, though? She required more. A lot more. While part of him rebelled at the obligation, some other part needed him to be the one who took care of her. Like no one else on Earth would do it right.

But that didn't make any sense, since he had no idea what protecting and caring for a human female entailed.

Great, as if he wasn't already on edge enough.

Melissa shucked her blouse and pulled on Cody's clothes with shaking fingers.

What had just happened?

She'd almost been taken. Except she knew Cody hadn't meant to hurt her. He'd half-shifted—teeth long, irises sky blue. She remembered that had happened to Ben before he marked Ashley, and he'd been devastated about what he'd done. Maybe this was why humans and shifters didn't mix.

What would've happened if she'd been a wolf? Or a *full* wolf, because she and Ashley were one quarter wolf. They hadn't known it, but their grandfather had been a shifter. After Ben had marked Ashley and she recovered more quickly than expected, they'd taken a road trip up to Wyoming to visit their Grandma Jane to uncover the family secret. She hadn't said much—the memory seemed painful to her—but she'd confirmed the man they knew as their grandfather hadn't sired her father. He'd been conceived by a shifter, whose pack had forced him to abandon her because she was human. He'd left her before he knew she was pregnant and she never made any attempt to tell him.

They told Grandma Jane about Ben, but the three had agreed to keep Ashley and Melissa's parents in the dark about it all unless there became a compelling need for them to know.

Would a full wolf have welcomed Cody's 'attack'? No, the situation never would have happened, because she would've known better than to run.

She slid her fingers through her tangled hair. Honestly, until she saw the lengthened teeth, she *had* wanted him. She would've parted her legs and let him plunge his huge cock—she was only guessing, but based on the size of the bulge in his jeans, it had to be—right into her core.

So what did the teeth mean? Surely he wasn't going to mark her. That would mean they were mated for life, and Cody didn't seem to even *like* her, apart from the sexual attraction between them.

Regardless of what it all meant, one thing had been confirmed—her instinct that this bad boy was as much trouble as her last boyfriend was dead on. She needed to keep her head, cross her legs, and wait this out. Soon, Ben and Ashley would be back and she could leave the protection of the silver wolf and find someone totally normal. And human.

Except those thoughts fell flat and thin as a crepe. She'd never be happy with normal, would she?

Sighing, she pushed open the bedroom door, the rumble in her empty stomach becoming more insistent than her desire to avoid Cody.

He stood at the stove, somehow managing to look both manly and incredibly sexy as he flipped something in a pan with a spatula. His broad shoulders rippled with muscle, and his torso tapered to a narrow waist followed by the best ass she'd ever seen on a man. There was something about those ripped, worn-out jeans.

Yum. Just yum.

She cleared her throat. "What are you making?"

The way he paused before speaking told her he'd known the whole time that she'd been standing there watching. Well, of course he had. He probably had extrasensory wolf instincts. She wondered what other gifts wolves possessed, apart from being able to jump from two-story windows, catch one hundred twenty-five pounds of falling woman, and drive a motorcycle like the 1970s hotshot Evel Knievel.

"Grilled cheese."

She snorted. "I should've figured that, Walmart boy." It was a low blow. Actually, she loved grilled cheese, but Cody had decided she was some kind of diva, so she figured she'd play the part just to goad him. It worked.

He whirled, brows down low over his eyes. "I didn't promise to feed you," he warned, with a shake of the spatula at her.

She smirked and sauntered forward, pretending he didn't look scary as hell. Backwards though it was, after what had just passed between them, she'd lost much of her fear of him. She'd seen his limits. "Keeping me alive probably involves feeding me, though, don't you think?"

His lips pressed together in a thin line. "Don't push your luck." He turned back to the stove and flipped a grilled cheese onto a plate beside a whole tomato. He thrust the plate in her direction, without turning to look at her.

She took it and looked down at the tomato, wondering how in the hell he expected her to eat it. Also, there was nowhere to eat. She hadn't noticed before, but he lacked a table and chairs. Rolling her eyes, she walked to the sofa and plopped down. No wonder it seemed dirty. This was where he must eat all his meals.

A moment later he joined her, sitting in the armchair across from her, his plate stacked with four grilled cheese sandwiches and two tomatoes.

Because she enjoyed needling him, she picked up the tomato. "How exactly do you expect me to eat this?"

The tic showed up in his jaw again. "I don't care how you eat it, or whether you eat it, princess. In fact, while you're here, maybe I should put you in charge of cooking." His eyes slid sideways and she caught the glint of goading in them. "I could use a live-in housekeeper around here."

That thought shouldn't turn her on. Especially not after living with Jeremy, who did absolutely nothing around the house. It must be the wicked way Cody looked at her that made her heart tumble and her flesh heat. She imagined wearing a little French maid's costume and running around to serve him under threat of a spanking while he waited with those powerful arms folded across his chest.

Stop it. Just stop. This guy was another Mr. Wrong. Definitely not the guy for her.

To throw it back at him, she held his gaze, picked up the tomato and took a big bite of it, as if it were an apple. Juice and seeds dribbled down her chin, but she didn't move to wipe them away.

Cody stared at her mouth, his expression turning hungry.

She jumped, pulse racing, when he leaped to his feet and stalked toward her.

"What are you doing to me?" he demanded in a guttural voice.

She froze, the tomato still gripped in her fingers in front of her mouth, juice dripping down her arm. She wasn't sure what he meant.

He grabbed the tomato out of her hand and then his mouth was upon hers. His tongue lapped up the juices before his lips descended on hers in a brutal kiss.

She gasped.

He hooked one hand behind her neck and hauled her to stand, body pressed against his, and took her mouth again and again.

Her nipples, bare beneath his oversized t-shirt, puckered and stood up, rubbing against the soft cotton.

When he broke away, he stared down at her like a man possessed. "Are you really sure you want to play that game with me?"

Dizzy with desire, she probably would have fallen over if he hadn't been holding her tight against his hard body.

She thought about playing innocent and asking "what game?" but they seemed beyond that. Cody had effectively put her on notice—nearly anything she did that might be construed as sexual put her in danger of getting fucked by him. And she bet he fucked hard and rough, like his manners.

She stared at his stubbled chin, not quite able to lift her eyes to his face.

The idiotic part of her wanted to wave the white flag and surrender. *Take me!* it cried, like the pathetic quick-bonding female she was.

Not going to happen.

She put her hands on his sculpted chest and pushed.

He moved back, but it was after a moment's hesitation, as if to show her that her feeble pushes meant absolutely nothing to a man—wolf—as strong as him. His eyes bored into her as if she stood there naked.

He brought the dripping fruit to her lips, offering it for another bite.

After his warning, she ought to have known better, but she sank her teeth into the soft meat of the tomato and closed her eyes with the explosion of taste, made all the more potent by her fascinated observer.

He ran his thumb over her lower lip, corralling tomato seeds into her mouth. "You're not going to last long around here."

"What do you mean?" Her voice only quavered a little. She licked the juice from her lower lip, missing being mashed up against his body. Despite the ill-fitting t-shirt and boxer shorts ensemble, she'd never felt so desirable in her life. Cody made every cell in her body spark to life, alert, simmering for his touch.

He gripped her hips, fingers firm against her flesh. "I'm already dying to bury my cock deep and pound until you scream my name."

Her mouth dropped open. She ought to be shocked by his crudeness, but dirty talk must be her thing because the flames of desire only burned hotter. Her breasts ached, swollen for his touch; her clit throbbed in time with her heartbeat.

"I-I can't," she somehow managed to stammer.

What she meant was she could. In a heartbeat. But it would be something her old self would do, and she was trying, very hard, to stop being the loser twin and do something right with her life for a change.

He released her and took a step back. Heat still burned in his gaze but as she watched, he produced an expression of scorn. "Then stay clear, princess, or you might find yourself in a compromising situation."

3

"I'm going to take a shower," Cody growled, stalking away from the tempting little human. *A cold shower.* Christ, what was it about her?

He shut the door to the bathroom with a resounding click and stripped off his work clothes. Ben Stone had seriously fucked up his life with this little alpha-to-alpha favor. He sure hoped it was worth it. With cold water on full blast, he climbed in, letting it pelt his body until the internal heat began to fade. He closed his eyes and rubbed a wet hand over his face, trying to erase the image of the way she'd looked with that tomato dripping down her chin.

That shouldn't have been so erotic. But there was something unique about this female that made her different from other humans. Maybe that's why Ben Stone had fallen for her sister. The fact that the powerful leader of the Denver pack—the billionaire CEO of a gaming company, who could certainly have his pick of any she-wolf in the world—had chosen a human said something.

He looked down at his cock, which still flew at half-mast. He'd better take care of it before he went anywhere near that human again, or there'd be trouble.

Fisting it, he leaned one hand against the tile and closed his eyes, allowing Melissa to screech into the forefront of his brain. Images flashed before his eyes—the flash of white thigh when her skirt had ridden up on the motorcycle; the way her arms fit around his waist so perfectly; her scent, intoxicating despite its humanness.

He pumped his aching cock and let the next batch of images flash through his brain. The dampness of her pink lace panties when he'd rubbed her clit, the flash of her pussy after he'd ripped them off. It had been shaved bare—for whom? That asshole of an ex-boyfriend? The thought made him grind his molars, the fingers on the tile wall curling into a fist.

He went back to replay the moment when he'd tossed her on the bed, on all fours, imagined what would've happened if she'd welcomed him—the look she might have tossed over her shoulder. A she-wolf would've bared her teeth, lowered her front haunches to give him her ass.

Yes… fuck, yes. He shot hot ribbons of cum against the tile wall, his eyes rolling back in his head with pleasure. Turning back into the stream of water, he rinsed off, noting that his cock still remained hopeful, despite the release.

Not going to happen, buddy. Get a grip.

MELISSA DREW several deep breaths to recover from the intensity of Cody's presence. His phone buzzed on the table and she glanced at it. Was Jeremy calling back? She shouldn't care about his welfare, but she couldn't help it. She picked it up, but the caller came up as 'Ed Smith.' Must be one of Cody's acquaintances.

She'd really like to call Ashley back and talk some more about this wolf stuff, but her phone was back at her apartment. So was her laptop.

If Cody was serious about her not leaving his place, she would need them, or else her business would take a huge dive, which she couldn't afford.

Her gaze wandered to his phone again. She wondered how long a shower he took. She could call an Uber car to drive her by her place. If it looked like the guys were still there, she'd just have the driver take her right back. But if it looked empty, she could run in and at least put together an overnight bag with the basic necessities. As much as she loved wearing Cody's shirt, she needed real clothes. And her toothbrush, and makeup, and—yes—her phone and laptop, dammit!

She downloaded the Uber app onto Cody's phone and logged into her account, which had her billing details already loaded. She quickly entered his address, which she got by poking her head out the door and checking the street sign and numbers on the house. It was a decent neighborhood, she realized. His property might be valued at twice what she originally estimated. Which was weird. Who bought a house in the Old North End and turned it into a workshop?

Yes! The Uber confirmed for just five minutes. This just might work. She could get away before Cody came out of the bathroom. Of course, there'd be hell to pay when she returned, but she was half excited about that, as crazy as it seemed.

Punishment from a sexy, dangerous wolf? Definitely something she'd like to experience at least once in her life. She'd always been the reckless twin, as Ashley liked to point out.

Hearing the car roll up outside, she slipped out. Her outfit was ridiculous, but she didn't care what the driver thought of her—this was an emergency.

She hopped in the car and the guy took off for her place, which was about fifteen minutes away.

It was a no-go, though. Lights lit up the place, and she could see the flicker of the television, and the dark silhouetted heads of two men sitting on the couch.

Damn.

"I'm not going to stop here," she said quickly to the driver as he started to park. "Take me back to the address where you picked me up."

He scowled in the rearview mirror. "That wasn't what you scheduled."

"I know. I'll add the additional ride in right now," she said, thumbing on her phone, her fingers flashing over the screen as she made good on her promise.

The driver grumbled, but took her back.

Her stomach dropped before the car even pulled up. A giant—seriously enormous—silver wolf sniffed the grass around the front steps. It jerked its head up and ice blue eyes stared right at her.

"Oh, my God, is that a wolf?" the driver asked. "Shut the door!"

"No, it's my dog. It's okay. Just a big husky. Not sure how he got out. Thanks, I'll add the tip to my card. Appreciate it!" She swung the door shut before he could mention the wolf again.

Then she swallowed and forced her feet to move in the direction of the front door—and the enormous wolf.

A low growl came from the wolf's throat and

she froze in her tracks. Was it Cody? What if it was some other, enemy wolf?

The wolf narrowed its eyes and sat down, as if waiting for her. Okay, angry wolf. Definitely Cody.

"Hi, Wolf. Silver. Big boy." Her voice only wavered a little. She turned the knob on the front door. The moment it swung wide, he pushed through, ahead of her.

Not really the gentleman, was he? It was probably a dominance thing. The alpha goes in first or some such rule. She thought she remembered that from that Cesar Milan dog training show. Not that she was comparing shifters to dogs.

She followed him in and shut the door behind him. He transformed before her eyes, shifting upright into human form, his magnificent male body stark naked, his cock jutting out at a perfect ninety-degree angle.

Her breath stalled in her throat. Whoa.

Damn.

As she'd suspected, his entire body was solid muscle. At least a dozen tattoos covered his body. Her mouth dropped open.

But she had an angry wolf on her hands. Irritation came off Cody in waves. His eyes hadn't changed back to gray yet, the cold blue gaze icy. He definitely wasn't angling for sex at the moment.

"Where in the hell did you go?"

She winced. "I took an Uber car to my place to

see if they'd gone. I really wanted my phone and laptop. The guys were still there, so I didn't stop." The words came tumbling out quickly, as she hoped to answer all his questions at once.

He glowered and stalked away to the bedroom, presumably to put some clothes on. A moment later, he returned in a pair of jeans, his torso still beautifully bare, apart from the ink. She admired the tattoos on his bulging biceps—they were beautiful designs and patterns, like crop circles or ancient symbols. She wondered what they meant.

"What did I tell you would happen if you left?"

She flushed as his graphic words returned to her. *I'll spank you until this perfect ass is red and your sweet little pussy is dripping wet.*

She couldn't decide if she hoped he'd follow through or not. She nibbled her lip. "I'm sorry, but I can't stay holed up here for days without my phone and computer. I have clients and a boss I need to communicate with. I can do a lot online—I might not even lose any business."

His nostrils flared and he drew a deep breath as if to calm himself. "Your career won't mean anything if you're dead. And I made an alpha's promise to keep you safe, which means if you'd been caught, your decision would seriously fuck my life up, too."

He stared at her for a long moment, his expression inscrutable. She realized his eyes had gone back to normal without her noticing when they'd changed. Then he held out his palm, as if to hold her hand. "Come here, princess. Time for your punishment."

He led Melissa to the side of the couch, pushed her torso over the arm, and gave her ass a smack. She sucked in a breath, but held her position, like she was interested in where this was going.

He slapped her ass again. He didn't want to hurt her—not in a way that wasn't sexual or didn't feel good. For a moment, he indulged in the idea of Melissa being his mate. He'd buy one of those furry, padded paddles and give her spankings that never hurt but were only symbolic of his dominance.

He rubbed a circle over her adorable butt, then peppered it with a couple more smacks. How far would she let him take this?

He peeled his boxer briefs down her heart-shaped ass. They were way too big for her and she'd rolled the waistband down several times, somehow managing to make them look both sexy and cute. The fact that she'd gone out in this outfit—alone with an Uber driver—made him grit his teeth, wanting to kill the driver for having seen her like this.

He gripped her wrists and twisted them behind

her back, pinning them with one hand as he dragged the briefs all the way off her with the other.

His cock strained at the sight of her naked ass, roaring to life, ready to sink between those beautiful thighs and never stop moving. He lifted his palm and let it fall. It landed with a crack on her right cheek.

She jerked, but didn't make a sound.

He repeated it on the left.

"When I tell you to stay put, you stay put," he growled, increasing the intensity of the spanks.

"*Bad. Girl.*" He spanked just a little harder.

She moaned, like being called a bad girl turned her on. Well, *hell yeah*. She could be his bad girl any day.

He drank in the sweet smell of her arousal.

His heart double-pumped when he realized his prediction had held true.

Her pussy really was dripping for him.

"I'm sorry. I won't do it again."

He stopped the onslaught and rubbed her cheeks, marveling at how soft her skin was. How much he loved seeing his handprints on her pretty ass. "Won't do what again?"

"I won't leave. I'll be good."

He liked the idea of her being his good girl even better.

Fuck. He needed to stop obsessing over this delectable human.

But he couldn't stop kneading her ass, squeezing her perfect flesh, not releasing her from the restraining position he'd put her in. He drew deep breaths in an effort to hold back the beast that screamed at him to throw her down and mount her in the most debasing way possible.

"Part your thighs if you want me to take care of that ache between your legs." His voice sounded gravelly.

She stilled, only her back rising and falling with the movement of her breath, her pretty face hidden from his view, turned into the cushions.

Damn..

Of course she wasn't going to offer herself up to him. What was he thinking? He'd just humiliated her. She probably wouldn't speak to him again.

To his shock, her feet inched apart.

He didn't move, not quite believing his eyes.

Her thighs opened wider, offering a clear view of the pink heart of her sex, dewy and plump.

A shudder of lust kicked through him. "Beautiful girl," he murmured, feeling as reverent as he sounded. Without releasing her wrists, he brought his fingers to her ripe core, running them lightly along her slit.

The way she humped the sofa arm nearly made him lose control. He stifled a curse and sought her clit. It was already swollen, hot beneath the pad of his finger. He circled once, twice, then flicked and tapped.

Her wanton cry made his hips jerk to match the movement of hers. He circled again. Flicked. Tapped.

"Cody…"

He loved the sound of his name on her lips way too damn much. He loved the scent of her arousal even more. He couldn't wait to taste her. Couldn't wait to hear what her cries sounded like when she came.

He slid his fingers down, seeking her welcoming entrance. They slid into her tight heat. He rotated them, angled his elbow to reach to the front of her wall, seeking her g-spot.

She squealed and bowed upward, her wrists pulling in his hand, her legs straightening, punished ass squeezing tight.

"Are you going to come for me, baby?" His voice didn't sound like his own; it had dropped two octaves.

"Yes," she moaned.

"Who are you going to come for?" He slid his fingers out of her and returned to her clit, circling, flicking.

Her thighs trembled, she humped relentlessly.

"You," she gasped.

He slapped her clit. "Say *please*."

"Please! Oh, God, please, Cody."

"That's it, baby, say my name. Who makes you come?"

"Cody! Cody makes me come."

He plunged his fingers inside her again and tickled her g-spot.

She screamed. Once more, she arched, her entire body tightening with her internal walls, which squeezed his fingers.

"Oh, my gawd! What did you do to me?" she wailed as her body continued to shudder and clench, her orgasm going on and on.

Her orgasm was even more spectacular than he anticipated. If he hadn't known what a fucking privilege it had been to witness, he might have lost control. He still could barely stand not claiming her. And yet he feared if he did, he'd mark her. She had an undeniable effect on him.

With a whimper, Melissa finally finished. He immediately scooped her into his arms and stood.

"I gotta put you out of reaching distance, princess," he muttered. "Before I do something I shouldn't." He carried her to his bedroom, pulled back the blankets and settled her on the mattress. She looked adorable in his oversized t-shirt and he had to work hard to ignore the screaming awareness that she wasn't wearing panties. With a flick of the blankets, he covered that tempting part of her anatomy.

He thought he ought to say something. The word *thanks* wasn't exactly appropriate since he hadn't been the one who got off, as his aching cock kept attesting. Probably *good night* would've summed it up, but his tongue didn't work—it was stuck to the roof of his mouth—so he simply turned off the light as he went out.

He would sleep on the couch. As fucking far away from that tempting little human as he could get.

MELISSA LAY ON THE BED, as limp as a rag doll. Her ass tingled. Pleasure still coursed through her in waves, but she felt the loss of Cody's presence acutely.

That was probably the hottest thing she'd ever experienced. He'd made her vulnerable, then rewarded her for it.

The stark intimacy of it all left her feeling raw. And then the way she'd shamelessly given herself over to him—not just that, but *begged* him to make her come—made her want to crawl in a hole.

She blinked into the darkness, all the emotions of the day catching up to her—from the terror of hiding in the closet, to the post-traumatic stress it brought up from her kidnapping a year ago, to the spanking and then the sex. If you could call that sex. Her orgasm. He hadn't gotten off, which surprised her. She hadn't pegged him for the kind of guy who cared about his partner's pleasure. At all.

She wanted to call Ashley, just to hear her twin, to talk about Cody and everything. Dammit, if she only had her phone!

Out of nowhere, a sob choked her. She didn't even know what it was about. She wasn't upset or mad. But all the emotion of the day came rushing to the fore. She sucked in deep breaths, trying to stifle it, but the more she did, the worse it got. Tears spilled from her eyes.

Oh damn.

Well, at least she hadn't broken down in front of Cody.

She didn't need to give that jerk any more ammunition. But *jerk* didn't fit. No jerk would take care of her needs without meeting his own. No jerk would carry her into bed and tuck her under the blankets like she was worth caring for.

Jesus, she was just so confused.

The door abruptly swung open and Cody strode in, looking dangerous.

She blinked, quickly mopping her cheeks.

"Fuck, Melissa. I'm sorry. Did I make you cry?" He sat down beside her and reached for her.

She didn't want him to see her crying. But when

she pushed against him, he caged her wrists in one large hand and scooped her onto his lap.

Funny how it instantly soothed her.

He tucked her trapped wrists against her chest and thumbed the tears off one side of her face.

She sucked in her breath.

"I'm an asshole. I'm sorry." He stroked the top of her head, down her neck, across her shoulder. Not in a sexual way like before. No, he was offering her comfort. His brand of it, apparently.

A snuggle. She was actually being cuddled by the dirty-talking tattooed bad boy who had just spanked her ass and put her to bed.

"No, it wasn't you. It was just everything. This is so embarrassing."

"Tears are a she-wolf's weapon," he murmured. "The scent of a female's tears makes her mate either go nuclear to protect her, or totally subdued to comfort."

She chewed on that, wondering what effect a human female's tears had on a wolf. But her thoughts couldn't keep up with the exhaustion of the day. She sank into Cody's embrace, leaning back, her head resting against his shoulder. Her eyes drifted closed, vague thoughts about how she ought to be furious with this overbearing shifter flitting through but taking no hold. Not when she felt so warm and safe for the first time since her kidnapping last year. Possibly for the first time in years.

She woke in the same position, still cradled half-upright against Cody's chest. The moment she stirred he brought his hand to her head, stroking her hair again. Or maybe he'd never stopped. She blinked at the illuminated clock on the bedside table. It was two a.m. Hours since she'd fallen asleep.

Had he slept at all? Or had he just been holding her like this the whole time?

Wanting to lie fully horizontal, she crawled out of his arms to the bed, curling up with her head on a pillow.

Cody dropped a kiss on her head then got up and left the room.

This time she felt the loss of him even more acutely. His warmth, his scent, though she'd never noticed a man's scent before. His was particularly pleasing—like leather and pine and strong, hard-working man.

She almost called after him—to tell him he could share the bed with her—but reason returned. That would be a bad idea. She'd already acted like a complete fool, opening her legs and begging him for an orgasm. And he'd made her.

Say my name. Who makes you come?

Even alone in the dark, she flushed at the memory. How had he reduced her to that wanton pleading woman? Stripped her of her pride and brought her right to the brink of ecstasy with just a few flicks of his fingers?

A man—wolf—like him had probably slept with hundreds of females to master that kind of skill. She was glad she'd escaped having sex with him. Never again. No, thank you. A guy like that… well, she was already half lost for him. The intensity of her attraction to him terrified her. She needed to take three steps back and squeeze her knees together real tight. No sex, no flirting. Definitely no more midnight cuddling.

Cody was the epitome of the kind of bad boy she always went for and this time, she was going to resist.

Somewhere out there a nice accountant or engineer would probably love an up-and-coming real estate agent girlfriend.

Somewhere, a nice, plain, boring guy wanted to sit on the couch and hold hands and watch *Mad Men* at night with her.

Why did that sound so incredibly awful?

4

Cody pushed open his front door quietly and carried in the bags from Walmart. The house seemed quiet, and his sensitive ears detected the slow sigh of breath from Melissa in the bedroom. Still asleep. He was glad—she needed it.

He'd slept less than an hour all night. When he'd smelled her tears from the bedroom the night before, he'd been horrified. If they'd come during the spanking, it would have been bad enough, but for her to cry after he thought he'd eased the tension between them—or at least her sexual tension—made him want to smack his head into a metal beam.

He didn't know the first thing about comforting a woman—had never tried it in his life, but the compulsion had been overwhelming. When she'd fought him off, confirming his fears that she'd never forgive him, he simply couldn't get up and walk away.

His mate was in need. He had to provide.

That was how it felt, anyway. But he didn't think of Melissa as a mate. Not even close. She was human, and not his type. They didn't even get along.

But the chemistry between them, or at least his for her, was off the charts. Once he'd comforted her, he'd been unable to sleep or even rest. Something about her nearness had his blood singing. His brain had gone around and around in circles—about his inexplicable attraction to her, about the trouble she was in, about how he might win her trust so she would follow his orders and he could keep her safe.

He wondered what her ex-boyfriend was like and he experienced violent thoughts toward the guy for putting her in this situation.

He put the milk and other staples in the refrigerator. Finding he had no idea what Melissa liked to eat, he'd stalled at the grocery store, then ended up buying everything in sight.

Behind him, he heard the rustle of movement from the bedroom and then the flush of the toilet. The door pushed open and the soft pad of bare feet sounded behind him.

He continued shoving groceries in the refrigerator to stall as he tried to figure out what to say.

When she didn't speak either, he turned and reached for one of the bags from Walmart. "Here are some clothes. I'm sure you'll hate them."

She reached for the bag. Somehow she managed to look even more beautiful with her hair all rumpled, her cheeks still stained with sleep. His eyes traveled to her lips, which looked bee-stung, swollen, and oh-so-kissable.

He tossed her a second bag. "There's a burner phone in there. And a Chromebook, so you can work."

Her jaw dropped. "You bought me a phone and computer?"

"Just a Chromebook."

"But I can't afford that," she said immediately, then blushed as if she didn't want him to know. Her words surprised him, although he should have gathered that from the location of her house. She had acted so stuck up that he'd assumed she came from money. But no, she was a wanna-be rich girl, the type who spent all her money to look rich, and fell into credit card debt to keep up appearances.

"Your brother-in-law can," he said gruffly. He wasn't sure why he didn't want to tell her it was no sweat off his back, that he had plenty of money and didn't mind buying her things. Possibly it was because she had been so stuck up about Walmart and his place. Like she'd been too good for him.

He didn't want to impress her with money,

because she was a superficial girl who cared about stuff like that.

There was a flaw in his logic, but he didn't care to tease it out at the moment.

She rolled her eyes and snatched the bags, opening them. She looked back up. "Thanks," she said grudgingly.

"What's missing?" He could tell she wanted to say something but had bit it back.

"Makeup," she mumbled.

He frowned. "You don't need that."

Her eyebrows lowered. "Whatever. You're the one who has to look at me."

He laughed. "What I see looks just fine, baby. More than fine."

Pink tinged her cheeks, making the blue of her eyes pop. Yeah, that girl did not need a drop of makeup.

"I got a bunch of food. I didn't know what you like to eat, but you should be able to find something. I gotta go get some work done."

She raised an inquisitive brow. "What kind of work?"

He hesitated. "Construction."

"Mmm." She looked properly unimpressed, as he'd expected. "Is there coffee?"

Damn, he hadn't thought of coffee. "No coffee," he grunted.

She stared at him in surprise, like he'd denied

her a basic right, like the use of a toilet or something.

"You'll have to suck it up, princess." He entered his number into her phone. "My number's in there. Call me if there's any trouble. Do I have to put a guard on the house, or are you going to stay put?"

Her eyes narrowed. "I'll stay put."

He stared her down for a beat, alpha style, but since she was human, she didn't quite get it. Her eyes never lowered, although an adorable blush did start to creep into her cheeks.

Though he knew it was unwise to get too close to her, he couldn't stop himself. He stalked around and leaned one hand on the table in front of her, bringing his face nose-to-nose with hers. "If you set foot out of this house, I'll spank your ass again," he warned in a low voice with a flick of his brows.

Her eyes dilated like she loved the idea. Well, that was one thing they had in common. He inhaled her scent before he walked away, and smiled when he detected the beautiful musk of arousal.

He headed out, calling Ben as he walked the few blocks to his current house project. He just had a few more rooms to paint and then molding to put on around the floors.

"This is Stone."

"Cody Steele. Checking to see if you found anything out on your end."

"My pack mate Mark Ruhl is DEA in Denver.

He knows the guy Rabago that you saw. Word on the street is that someone stiffed Rabago on a huge shipment to Colorado Springs. He's coming down to question Melissa, but he already has an APB out on Jeremy, her dickwad ex-boyfriend. Best guess, Jeremy or one of his friends was behind the bad drug deal and they think he has the money. I'm willing to pay it off to get the hit off Melissa, but we need a plan to contact him and make the offer. Do you have any connections to this guy?"

"None." His pack mates weren't angels, but he'd helped most of them become semi-contributing members of society. He'd know if any of them were into anything that deep.

"Okay, I'll keep working on my end. You just keep Melissa safe, and try to get your hands on her asshole ex."

The alpha in him bristled at Stone giving him orders, but then he experienced a stab of doubt about leaving her alone at the house. Maybe he should've put a guard on her.

"What are you doing with a human wife, Stone?" he blurted.

"Fuck you."

"No, really. I want to understand." He sounded rude, but he couldn't explain to Ben Stone that he found his sister-in-law utterly intoxicating. He just had to know if Ben had felt the same about Melissa's sister. Had he wanted to mate her right from the start?

"She's part wolf," Ben growled.

Cody stopped halfway up the walk to the house he was working on. "She is? Melissa too?"

"They're twins," Ben said drily and it pissed him off he didn't know that. He didn't know anything about her, really, and that annoyed him, too. He didn't plan to have this conversation with Ben, though. He'd ask Melissa, for fuck's sake.

He unlocked the door to the house and headed in to prep the house for paint.

Knowing she was part wolf changed everything. Explained everything. There wasn't something wrong with him—she had wolf blood that sang his song. It still didn't make her a worthy choice for a mate. He needed a she-wolf who could produce pups, not human babies. But at least he understood the attraction now.

He stretched out the drop cloth and shook a can of paint, wondering if he'd bought anything she liked for breakfast. That was stupid. He shook his head to clear it of thoughts of her. What did he care if she liked what he bought? It wasn't like he was courting her.

～

MELISSA MADE AN OMELET FOR BREAKFAST. She followed it up with a fruit smoothie, since Cody had bought fresh blueberries, raspberries, and strawberries. Funny, she didn't think a guy like him would buy fresh berries. He seemed like the boxed cereal and canned meals type. Were they for her?

She didn't want to cancel any of her appointments that week, nor her volunteering commitments with Big Brothers Big Sisters, but she couldn't see any way around it. She called into the office on the burner phone and told them she was going to work from home because she had a sore throat. It rang again just as she finished eating. She wasn't sure if she should pick up, but then she recognized her sister's number.

"Hey, how's it going? Cody texted Ben your new number."

That was nice of him.

"Did you survive the wolf domination?"

She snorted. "Okay, first of all, you weren't kidding. He spanked me!"

Ashley laughed. "Are you okay? Did you…"

"What?"

"Have sex with him?"

She choked on her smoothie, spraying it across the kitchen table. Grabbing a napkin, she mopped the dribbles. "Not exactly." Her voice sounded strangled.

"What happened?" Only a twin would have zero boundaries with demanding every dirty detail.

"He, um, brought me to orgasm." She laughed.

"Nice. Was it good?"

Why was she blushing when her sister couldn't even see her face?

"It was good." That wasn't true. It had been spectacular. Cody had done more with his fingers than any guy had done with his mouth, fingers, or manhood. The orgasm had been explosive.

"Just good? What aren't you telling me? Did you hate the dominance? Is that why you're upset?" Ashley probed.

"I'm not upset. What makes you think I'm upset?"

"Maybe that's not the right word, but your voice is all tight like there's something you're not saying."

"I've got guys trying to kill me, I'm being held semi-prisoner by a wolf who spanks, and I can't meet with clients or show houses, so I may miss out on some important deals. Is that enough to make my voice tight?"

"It's something about Cody. I know it is."

Damn. Sisters were hard to fool.

"He's hot. And grumpy. He unnerves me. I can't quite figure him out. One second I decide he's a cocky redneck laborer and the next he's comforting me or doing something thoughtful and all the while he's turning me on, making overt sexual come-ons that should totally piss me off, but instead have me soaking my panties. It's just all too much. I don't know what to do with it."

"Wow. I wish I'd met him. I don't know whether to advise you to stay the hell away from him or not."

"I think I should keep my panties on and my legs crossed. He's got the same kind of appeal as Jeremy, and you know how badly that went."

"Ugh. Yeah, I do. Then you're probably right. Steer clear. Don't provoke his dominance, because sexy times will just complicate things."

"I've arrived at the same conclusion."

"Ben's working on this end to get things figured out with that asshole who's after Jeremy. He will pay him off or his buddy will arrest him. Either way, they're taking care of it, 'kay?"

She exhaled, releasing some of the stress she'd been carrying around. "Thanks, I feel a little better. I'm sorry if this is ruining your honeymoon."

"No, it's fine. I'm on the beach getting a tan and drinking a banana daiquiri, but if you want us to come back, we'll be on the next plane home."

"No. Please, stay. Hey, Ash?"

"Yeah?"

"I don't want Jeremy to get killed. Could you tell Ben and his friends that? I know they don't give a crap about him, and this is his fault and everything, but…"

"What, you still feel like you owe him something for saving your life?"

"Yeah." She knew Ashley would get it.

"Okay, I'll relay the message. Take care of yourself."

"You too. Have fun with that wolf of yours."

"I will. *Hasta luego, hermana.*"

Melissa laughed at the horrible accent. Her sister's Spanish sucked. "Talk to you later. Love you."

She hung up smiling and flipped open the Chromebook Cody had bought her. It was surprisingly easy to set up and in no time at all, she had accessed her email and listings. Maybe working from Cody's wouldn't be all that bad, so long as she could conduct all business over the phone, rather than in person.

And working in her pajamas wasn't half bad either, although she was ready for a shower. She stood and stretched, grabbed the bags of clothes Cody bought, and headed to the en suite bathroom.

Like the rest of Cody's place, the bathroom could use a good cleaning. She wrinkled her nose at the mold growing in the corners of the tile and the ring around the tub.

Nasty. She wasn't setting foot in that thing until it had been disinfected at least three times.

She looked under the sink and found cleaning supplies. With a pair of rubber gloves pulled up to her elbows, she broke out the Ajax and got on her hands and knees with a scrub brush.

An hour later she deemed the bathroom passable, and took her shower. Of course, the shampoo was total crap and there was no conditioner. Plus, she hated—*hated*—deodorant soaps. *Yuck*. Now she would smell like sudsy grass all day.

She stepped out of the shower and wrapped a towel around her body before dumping the bags of clothing on Cody's bed.

She snorted when she picked up a four-pack of the ugliest set of pastel granny panties she'd ever seen. He must've been joking with those. Maybe he was hoping it would kill the attraction between the two of them. Oh wow, purple leggings. She laughed out loud when she saw the tanktop that read *Princess* in fuchsia across the boobs. "Very funny, wolf man," she muttered.

Some normal stuff was in the pile, too. He'd bought jeans in a size five and seven—she supposed he didn't know which size would fit her. Several solid colored t-shirts and cute cotton panties that actually might fit. Nothing she would ever buy on her own, but it was better than wearing his shirt and boxer shorts.

She held up a very long pair of black and white witch socks that would probably serve as thigh-highs. He must've bought this stuff on purpose to goad her.

Perfect. If that's what he wanted to see her in, she'd give him a show.

~

CODY UNLOCKED the front door and pushed it open. And then stopped dead. Melissa was scrubbing his kitchen floor on her hands and knees wearing… *holy shit.*

He swallowed, his body temperature rising five degrees just looking at her. Melissa wore a pair of black and pink panties, which tragically covered most of her ass, but the backs of her thighs flashed bare above the long black and white socks he'd bought.

She turned and stood up on her knees, looking over her shoulder like a pinup star. On top she wore the *Princess* tank top with no bra, the peaked tips of her nipples plain through the thin fabric. She'd pulled her hair into pigtails—pigtails, dammit—and she rocked the Harley Quinn *Suicide Squad* thing to a tee.

He groaned, readjusting his cock in his jeans to ease the ache.

She twirled one pigtail and affected an innocent voice. "Were these the clothes you wanted to see me in, Cody?"

His mouth went dry. He backed against the door, not trusting himself to get anywhere near her.

"I warned you what would happen if you played this game, didn't I?" His voice rasped scratchy and low, hands tightened into fists at his sides, fingernails dug into his palms.

"It's clearly your game. You dressed me."

"You're going to get yourself fucked so hard you'll forget your own name."

She stood up, lifting her chest, the perky tips of her breasts pointed directly at him. "You bought the clothes."

Well, she was right about that. Except he'd bought them as a joke. Never in a million years had he imagined she would turn them into a sex kitten getup that would keep him perma-hard.

Do not move from this door. He willed his body to stay in place.

"You have three seconds to run for the bedroom and lock the door. Don't come out until you've changed into…" he cleared his throat, "something I can handle seeing you in."

She didn't move, her blue eyes wide.

"Stay here and I'll have you bent over the arm of that sofa with my cock buried between those fucking gorgeous thighs in less than five. *Go.*"

She edged sideways, keeping her eye on his face. When she reached the bedroom, she threw herself inside and slammed the door. Not until the rattle of the handle told him she'd locked the door did he breathe.

He stabbed his fingers through his hair. *Fucking hell.*

"Don't come back out," he yelled at the door. *Not for a week, at least.* He didn't know how he'd get rid of his raging hard-on. He rubbed a hand over his eyes, trying to erase the image of her scrubbing the floor in that outfit, which had been permanently burned on his retinas. He wanted her so badly.

He stared at the bucket and scrub brush on the floor for a long time before he realized she had actually been cleaning. That hadn't just been for show. A quick glance around his place revealed vacuumed carpets, dusted surfaces, papers straightened into neat piles. Even the furniture had been vacuumed.

Well, I'll be damned.

He wasn't sure how to reconcile the hardworking housecleaner with the stuck-up snob who sneered at clothes from Walmart.

She'd busted her ass to clean his house, which he appreciated. He had to admit he didn't do a good job around his own place. If he lived with other people, he would pull his own weight, but since it was just him, it hardly mattered. He spent all day fixing up houses for other people, making them perfect. He didn't feel that inspired about doing it for himself. But now, seeing his place through her eyes, he cringed. It had been pretty bad. Certainly not the place you'd bring a girl to impress her.

But he'd done absolutely nothing to impress this girl, had he?

He headed out the back door to fire up the grill. He'd bought a couple of steaks and the idea of cooking for her after she'd cleaned his place suddenly seemed important.

"You can come out now," he called out when he returned, pulling the steaks out of the refrigerator and slapping them on a plate to douse with seasoning and Worcestershire sauce. "*If* you've put something else on," he added hastily.

She emerged, dressed in a pair of jeans and a bold, hot pink t-shirt. He winced. "I see."

She folded her arms across her chest. She had a bra on this time, saving him from the pain of staring at her nipples. "What do you see?"

"I should have let you pick out your own clothes." She still looked hot—because clothes didn't make or break a female like her—but the outfit didn't fit her right; the jeans were too big and the shirt too small.

She laughed softly, a gorgeous smile lighting up her face.

"Come here, Melissa." He crooked a finger, half expecting her to tell him to fuck off.

She didn't, though, and the swing of her hips as

she sauntered over undid all the effort he'd put into calming his raging libido.

He caught one of her wrists and spun her toward the kitchen counter, placing her hand, along with its mate, on the edge of the countertop. "Spread your legs, baby," he murmured in her ear.

Shockingly, she obeyed.

He brought his hand down hard on one jean-clad cheek.

She gasped, but didn't break position.

He smacked the other side, just as hard. "You know what that's for, princess," he growled. With far less force, he brought his palm up to spank her pussy.

"Oh!"

He shoved his hips up against hers, reaching around and rubbing the seam of her jeans against her clit. "Thank you for cleaning my house," he murmured against her ear, then nipped it with his teeth. "That was nice of you. I'm sorry it was a mess."

He didn't often apologize, and it wasn't easy, especially not with her. Fortunately, she didn't get high and mighty on him. Of course, she may not have even heard, because his finger kept working the seam of her jeans right up against her clit and she squirmed against him, her breath coming in quick sharp pants.

"I found out why you smell so good for a

human." He licked along the shell of her ear. "You have some wolf blood in you."

"Does that turn you on?" The husky purr of her voice nearly made his cock turn bionic as it tried to punch right through his jeans to nail that sweet little ass she kept grinding against him.

His vision domed but he drew deep breaths to keep the beast at bay. "How long do you think it would take me to make you orgasm right here, with those jeans still on your hot little body?"

She trembled beneath him, grinding her pussy on his fingers. When she didn't answer, he gave her mons another slap. "Hmm?"

"I don't know," she moaned. She sounded close. Very close.

He slid his hand up under her shirt and kneaded her breast. "Thirty seconds? More?"

She reached back and grasped his neck, digging her nails into his skin. The she-wolf move made him roar as once more the beast surged to the surface, so ready to mark her.

He rubbed his knuckle over her clit, slapped her pussy hard and fast.

She squealed, yanking on his neck, hanging from it as her legs gave way.

With another firm grind of her jeans into her clit, he growled, "Come for me, baby."

She snapped. Her hips bucked wildly and he had to hang on tight to keep the pressure where it counted. Her head thrown back on his shoulder, she scratched at the back of his neck, cried out over and over again while her entire body shuddered with release.

His own body trembled, the effort of holding back his desire so great. He whirled her around, pinned her back against the cabinets. His eyes had changed color, he knew by the way she stared up at them, fear and fascination warring in her expression.

"You… shouldn't do that," she said breathlessly. Even though she was right, it offended him. He wanted her sighing his name, falling against him with blissful gratitude.

But of course that wouldn't happen. Not with Melissa and the lofty standards he'd never meet. With great willpower he pushed away from her and stepped back.

He grabbed the plate of steaks and stalked out to the backyard to throw them on the grill.

LIKE THE LAST time Cody had brought her to climax and then abruptly left her, she felt unmoored. Her body missed his heat, his masculine scent, his growly voice hot in her ear. Her clit throbbed, raw after his torture.

He'd seemed offended as he stalked away.

What was he trying to prove? That he could control her as easily with sex as he could with the threat of punishment? Or could he just not help himself?

She secretly hoped it was the latter.

She'd seen the blatant hunger on his face when he first came in and saw her getup. His hands had closed into fists and he'd stayed glued to the door, as if he feared getting too close to her.

She opened the refrigerator and pulled out the fixings for salad, automatically getting to work as her mind turned over her six foot four inches of solid trouble.

Maybe this was the wolf form of courtship— hot sexual encounters littered with threats of far worse. And she'd rejected it with her warning after she climaxed. Which was probably why he'd stalked away, that tic in his jaw showing she'd succeeded once more in irritating him.

Their exchanges had almost become a game to her. Except it wasn't one she was sure she wanted to win. Not if it meant Cody thought her a heartless bitch who only cared about herself, which she knew was how she came off.

But she didn't need to show him her real self, either. This wasn't a relationship—she'd already decided it couldn't go anywhere.

By the time she finished putting two salads on

plates, Cody returned with the cooked steaks, still looking pissed.

"Mmm, that smells heavenly," she said in an attempt to ignore the tension between them.

"So you do eat meat?" he asked gruffly.

She wasn't sure if it was another innuendo. Was he complaining that she hadn't reciprocated with a blowjob yet?

She darted a sidelong glance at him and settled for an ambiguous, "Yep."

He glanced at the plates she'd set out. "Thanks for making salad." He sounded grudging, like it cost him to thank her for anything, or like manners were unfamiliar territory. It tugged at her heart. Was he actually making an effort to be polite?

"Thanks for the steak." She tried to keep her voice light and friendly.

He added steak knives to their place settings and sat down on the sofa with her. "How much blood?"

She knew what he was asking—about her wolf heritage. "A quarter. My grandmother got involved with a wolf in Cheyenne. He had to leave her because she was human, and he never knew she was pregnant."

Cody frowned. "Your grandmother couldn't find him to tell him?" Surprise crinkled the lines of his forehead.

She stabbed a piece of steak with her fork and popped it in her mouth. "Mmm."

Cody stopped eating, staring at her lips as she chewed.

"This is heavenly."

He seemed to forcibly look down at his own plate for a bite of steak.

"She didn't try. She said his pack made him leave her, so she didn't want to interfere. He'd already made his choice."

Cody wiped his mouth with a napkin. For some reason, she found herself surprised by how refined and cultured his table manners were. She'd assumed him to be a sort of redneck, but instead, he'd placed his napkin in his lap straightaway, chewed with his mouth closed, and ate neatly for such a big, hungry man. Not huge feats, but ones that neither Jeremy, nor any of the guys she'd dated in the past, had managed.

"It would've changed things," he said matter-of-factly. "She should've told him. A wolf takes care of his own."

Curiosity flickered, curling in her chest. She wanted to know how a wolf took care of his own, not in the hypothetical sense, but specifically, how a playboy wolf like Cody, who seemed terminally single, would take care of a female if he accidentally got her pregnant. She shook her head to clear that errant thought from her mind. Where were these thoughts coming from?

Cody went on, "He would've protected his female and that pup with his life, provided for both of them. Whose father was he? Your mother's or your father's?"

"My father's."

She swallowed another bite of savory meat. Cody had seasoned it and just seared the outside, so the rare meat melted in her mouth. She found herself vaguely surprised that he knew how to cook a gourmet steak, expecting him to be more of the type to drown it in barbecue sauce—or God forbid —ketchup. Instead, he'd produced better steak than she'd find at the best Colorado steakhouse.

"Your dad never shifted?"

"No, and he doesn't know. Ashley and I didn't find out until Ben marked her."

Cody watched her lips again, that look of hunger flickering on his face before he dragged his eyes to meet hers. "What happened?"

Part of her didn't want to tell him, it was Ashley and Ben's story, after all. But some part she didn't want to examine too closely thought he should know—that he needed to know, in case it became relevant for… them.

"It happened accidentally. Ben lost control and bit her here." She indicated the place where neck met shoulder, remembering the horrific marks on her sister right after he'd done it. "She recovered much faster than they expected, which led one of his pack mates to question whether she had wolf blood. We realized we're never sick or hurt and our father used to brag he'd never been sick a day in his life. Also, that the father line is blank on his birth certificate. So Ashley and I drove up to Wyoming to ask our Grandma Jane, and she told us her story."

"Wyoming, huh? What's his name?"

She shook her head. "She didn't tell us. Why, do you know wolves in Wyoming?"

Cody nodded. "Yeah. The wolf community is small." He'd finished his steak and salad and now he wiped his mouth again and set his fork and knife on the plate, like he was at a restaurant. "The Wyoming pack is coming to Estes Park next month for the annual games. Maybe you should go."

She gaped in surprise. "Are you going?"

A muscle in his jaw jumped. "No. It's my father's gig, and we don't get along."

She filed that information away to chew on later. Somehow it didn't surprise her that he didn't get along with his dad. Even though he must be nearing thirty years old, he carried that 'rebel' vibe like a badge.

It was in her nature to serve, even a male who didn't deserve it, so she stood, picking up both their plates from the coffee table and carrying them to the kitchen. Without checking, she knew Cody's heated gaze followed her and she had to admit she loved it. She'd never been with a guy who made her feel so desirable. The fact that Cody seemed unable to control his desire—despite his obvious dislike for her—gave her a sense of pleasure and power.

5

Cody put the gun in the waistband of his jeans again. "Come on, princess."

Melissa had just finished hand-washing all the dishes, a sight that nearly undid him. Her acts of domesticity made him harder than stone. Hell, everything about her made him hard. But her willingness to pitch in pleased him, and not because he cared about those things.

It went against his initial impression that she was just a spoiled stuck-up human. But also something more primitive approved—his inner wolf found it proof she was mate-worthy.

Too bad his inner wolf was wrong.

A quarter wolf still meant three-quarters human. He'd grown up in Estes Park, Colorado, where the entire mountain town was made up of shifters. He hadn't had to deal with humans. Even after being kicked out at age sixteen, he'd stuck with his own kind. Apart from random gratuitous sex with human females, he didn't find them good for much. And his father's parting taunt had made him certain he'd rather die single than mate a human and prove his father right.

Melissa turned from where she was wiping down the countertops for the second time—who double-wiped down countertops? He wondered if she did that after every meal.

"Where are we going?"

"To the mall to buy you some clothes."

Surprise flickered over her face. "Oh." Then her expression clouded. "Listen, I don't have my purse, so I don't have my credit cards or anything."

"I'll take care of it." He didn't put it off on her brother-in-law this time. He was starting to get the idea she didn't ask for money from him, which he could understand.

She arched a dubious brow and annoyance flashed through him. She thought he couldn't afford it. If she knew he had a half million dollars sitting in the bank and close to another two-and-a-half million currently tied up in properties, she might not act so snobby around him. But he didn't want to impress her with his money, mainly because she was exactly the type who *would* be impressed. Somehow, her superficial snobbiness made him want to be relentlessly himself—rough, crude, and blue collar.

"Aren't you worried about me being seen out?"

He held open the front door. "A little. But I'll be with you."

She walked past him and turned up her little button nose. "You have a pretty high level of confidence in yourself, don't you?"

He slapped her ass as he followed her out. "That's why I'm alpha, baby."

She snorted, then halted on the sidewalk, staring at the CJ Steele Construction lettering on his pickup. "You work for CJ Steele?"

He only hesitated for a moment before answering smoothly, "Yep." It was not a lie. He was Cody Jack Steele—only he went by Cody, not CJ. So, yes, he owned the company and certainly worked for himself.

She swiveled her gaze to him, something akin to awe shining in her eyes. "Really? You restore the Old North End houses?"

He tried to ignore the fierce pleasure her admiring tone stirred. It must be his inner wolf, still angling to get laid by the leggy human. "Yeah."

"Wow. What's it like? Does he direct the vision and his workers execute? Or is there a formula… like a stylebook you use? How long have you worked for him?"

Annoyance over the fact that she assumed he was some menial laborer on the projects warred with appreciation for her excitement. He thought his company did good work, and the market seemed to think so, as well, but the reverential way she spoke made him feel like a goddamn hero.

"I've been with the company pretty much since the start." He held the door open for her, mainly because he knew she didn't think he had it in him. "Steele directs it all, I guess."

He walked around and sat in the driver's seat.

"My first deal as an agent was with CJ Steele." She sounded rueful. "I got my ass handed to me."

Her uncharacteristic humility fascinated him and he watched her flush at the memory while he started the truck. "What do you mean?"

She shrugged. "I lost the deal. A huge one—a half a million dollar home. It was horrible—I'd been so proud of getting my license and thought I was finally going to make something out of myself and then I totally screwed it up."

He didn't like hearing her talk that way about herself. *Finally* going to make something of herself? She didn't strike him as a fuck-up like he'd been. Apart from her poor choice in a boyfriend, that is.

He struggled to remember a deal falling through, but there'd been so many and he didn't know the time frame.

"I missed the inspection and Steele yanked it from us. He probably had a better offer and was just waiting for me to mess up." Again, she sounded rueful, rather than bitter. He definitely didn't remember yanking a house from a buyer because he had a better offer, but a deal had fallen through six or seven months ago due to an inspection.

"*Steele* yanked it?"

She shrugged. "That's the tough thing about real estate. You can never tell if it's the agent who's the hard-ass or the guy behind him. I like to think it was the agent."

His lips twitched. "Why's that?"

"I love Steele's work. I admire the hell out of him and what he's done in this town in just a few short years."

"Huh." Irrational pleasure spiked through him.

"I'm dying to own a CJ Steele home—they're so beautiful." The respect and awe in her voice made his chest ache, which didn't make any damn sense. It couldn't be because he wanted her to feel that admiration for him, Cody, instead of the Steele she'd put on some pedestal.

He parked at the Promenade Shops at Briargate and looked balefully out at the scene. He'd rather have tacks shoved under his fingernails than go clothes shopping. He wished he could just hand Melissa a wad of cash and wait in the car for her, but that wouldn't be safe. He glanced at the clock on the dash.

"You have forty-five minutes to find what you need."

Her eyes widened as if shopping that quickly was an impossibility. "Why? What's the rush?"

"That's when my patience for this," he made an irritated gesture toward the shops, "expires. And believe me, you don't want to find out what happens when I expire." He figured he sounded like a grumpy asshole, but Melissa giggled.

Seeing the brightness of her smile nearly took his breath away. Angelic. It made him want to make her laugh again, but he couldn't think of anything funny to say. Instead his lips surprised him by stretching into a matching smile.

Their gazes tangled, lingering too long until he forced himself to shove the truck door open and tumble out.

Melissa headed straight for the Anthropologie store, her walk brisk. Apparently she'd taken the time limit as a challenge. He grinned and followed her, eyes on her heart-shaped ass.

She worked efficiently, seeming to know what she wanted, and plucking clothes from the rack with a determined air. He stayed by the doorway, arms folded across his chest. Based on the looks people threw him, he stood out. Well, he was used to that. The tattoos and rough appearance drew wary glances wherever he went. Still, it seemed to underscore the differences between him and Melissa, which for some reason pissed him off.

He had no interest in Melissa. No interest apart

from prying those creamy white thighs open and fucking her hard and fast until she begged to come. Why should he give a rat's ass if they were compatible? It wasn't like they were entering into a relationship.

Except he knew most of that was a lie. His wolf wanted her, for a need beyond sex.

Mate.

He swore softly under his breath, catching another nervous glance from a customer.

He wasn't going to mate a human. Especially not a stuck-up brat like this one. But the memory of her face lit up by that smile flashed in his mind and he felt himself softening again. That smile had been genuine, the real Melissa. The girl who'd let him hold her the night before after he'd made her cry. That girl... he needed.

MELISSA TRIED to make quick mental notes of the basic clothing she might need. A couple of casual things, something suitable for work, just in case. Underclothes. Sleepwear. She didn't want to spend too much money—she didn't have much in her bank account to use to reimburse Cody, which is why she would have preferred using her credit card.

She kept her eye on the time, not because she was worried about Cody 'expiring' but because she loved a challenge. Eighteen minutes. She took the clothes she'd found and headed out, catching Cody's eye. She hated him having to cover this. She didn't know how much he had, but being a burden on him didn't sit well with her.

He started toward her, his movement far more fluid and graceful than she'd expect on such a large, muscled man. But he wasn't just a man. She remembered the silver wolf sniffing outside for her the night before—huge, threatening. Magnificent.

He stuck his hand in his pocket and withdrew a wad of bills, just as she'd expect from a guy like him. No wallet. No credit cards. Just a huge wad of cash. Kinda like Jeremy. Did that mean he was into illegal things like Jeremy? Why was he carrying so much cash?

He grabbed a purse from a nearby rack and tossed it on the counter.

She lifted a brow and he shrugged. "You need one, right?"

She bit her tongue to keep from saying, *yeah, but not that one.* He already thought she was a picky bitch. Scanning the others on the rack, she quickly traded it out before the cashier rang it up.

Cody paid for it all—*gulp*—two hundred and eighty dollars' worth of stuff. He dropped a hand on her nape as they walked out. "It's okay, baby. Are you worried you have to pay me back?"

Had it shown on her face? She didn't like being

dependent on him like this. She squared her shoulders and lifted her chin. "No, I can afford it. I just need to get access to my stuff." Her voice came out slightly higher pitched than usual.

He contemplated her for a moment and she felt stripped bare, like he saw right past her lie. He stopped, the hand at her neck holding her back as he pulled her around to face him. Tilting her chin up, he rumbled in his deep voice, "I'm taking care of it." A wicked light gleamed in his eyes. "But you're welcome to show your appreciation for your sugar daddy any way you please."

Her lips curved when she caught the raw hunger in his expression. Remembering the power she'd felt at tempting him that afternoon, she ran her fingers across his chest, tracing the lines of his chiseled muscles. "Is that so?" she purred, using a honeyed voice and lowering her lids to half-mast. "Right here? In the mall?"

His eyes changed to light blue. "Careful," he rasped, his voice two octaves deeper than normal. He burrowed his fingers into her hair and wound it around his fist, tugging her head back at the same time he yanked her flush against his body. The insistent bulge of his erection pressed against her belly. "You think I won't find a way to fuck you raw, right here, in the mall?" He laughed harshly. "I'm a very resourceful wolf when I'm offered a challenge."

Her mouth went dry, heat descending from her

core down her inner thighs. When she moistened her lips with her tongue, his eyes fastened on it, body stiffening.

"Cody." Her voice sounded shaky. "People are looking."

Some of the wildness left his face and he relaxed, but still held her in position against him. "You should've thought of that before you pulled a cock tease." His eyes changed back to gray. He bent his head and to her shock, kissed her. Not a sweet, gentle kiss, but a marauding, violent one.

She held still for it, her insides fluttering, as his tongue swept between her lips and he bit and sucked at them, repositioned his angle and did it again.

When he released her, it was all at once—the hand from her hair let go, he lifted his head from hers and stepped back.

She swayed on her feet, dizzy from the kiss, breathless. Trembling.

"I'll have to punish you for that," he muttered and this time there was no mistaking the excitement his words produced. Her pussy clenched, liquid heat poured down her legs.

God, yes.

Cody's nostrils flared and his head whipped around, his gaze on a tense, worried-looking mother and her two children who hurried past them. The little girl, who appeared around seven or eight, craned her neck to look back at Cody until her mom tugged her arm, rushing her on.

"Do you know them?"

Cody frowned. "No."

She waited, because *no* was not a sufficient enough explanation for the way both he and the girl had stared at each other.

"They're shifters. I've never seen them before."

"Oh." She blinked in surprise. "You could… smell them?"

"Yeah."

"Is it unusual? Are you supposed to say hi or something?"

He flashed an uncharacteristic grin at her, as if he found her amusing, or cute. "Yeah. This is my town, I'm alpha. If she lives here, she should've sought me out to introduce herself."

"Maybe she just hasn't had a chance?" But even as she said it, she realized the woman gave the distinct impression she was trying to get away from Cody before he noticed her.

Cody shrugged, but appeared troubled. "We'll see." He pulled out his phone and glanced at it. "You have nine minutes left."

"What?" she cried indignantly. "You can't count that time we were…"

He folded his arms across his chest. "Can't I?"

With a wild glance up and down the row of

stores, she took off briskly for the Ann Taylor Loft, where she planned to get a business outfit.

"Damn, I was hoping you were going to go there," Cody muttered, lifting his chin toward the Victoria's Secret.

"Yeah, I'll bet." She didn't break her stride. "You probably thought I'd give you a show."

"Hey, you think it's fun to rouse the wolf. You're the one who will be sorry when she's spread-eagle on her back in the middle of the mall."

This time, she knew he didn't mean it, he was just getting a rise out of her. The man—wolf—was so incredibly crude. She ought to hate the filthy way he talked to her, but the words sent flames of desire licking up her core. And while everything he said was dominant and demeaning, the idea that she sparked such desire in him made her feel powerful.

He slapped her ass, his long legs making it easy for him to keep up with the brisk pace she'd set. She rushed in and picked out two blouses and a skirt. Cody stepped forward and paid for them.

"Ready?"

She'd been hoping to buy some shoes, because she only had her dress shoes and the sneakers Cody picked up at Walmart, but she'd spent enough money already. "Yeah. Thanks." She stood on her tiptoes and gave him a peck on the cheek, which again, he seemed to find cute.

6

Cody let Mark Ruhl, the burly DEA agent from Denver, into his place that evening.

"I'm sorry I couldn't make it sooner, we had a big bust go down last night and it took all day to wrap up the paperwork." He shook Cody's hand and stepped inside. "Hi, you must be Melissa." He shook her hand, as well. "We met at Ben and Ashley's wedding but you probably don't—"

"I remember you," she chirped, flashing that megawatt smile that made his insides rattle.

Cody's fingers closed into fists at his sides. She'd better not remember him with any particular fondness or he'd… He closed his eyes and attempted to rein in the snarling beast within.

She's not your mate.

Except that assertion only made him want to smash the friendly DEA agent's face even more. His inner wolf raged to mark her, not paying any attention to the fact that Cody didn't even like the girl, and would never in a million years mate a human.

"Can I get you a beer?"

"Sure. Okay if I sit?" Mark headed to the sofa and Melissa trailed behind, too close for his sanity.

He walked to the refrigerator to get three Budweiser bottles out.

Maybe he should just have sex with her and get her out of his system. The chemistry was there, whether they liked each other or not. Her body responded every time he touched her, almost like she couldn't help herself. Maybe that was why she'd cried the night before after he'd pleasured her. She hadn't wanted to give him that.

That idea made him gnash his teeth and want to put his fist through a wall. He would never force himself on a female and the idea that she *hadn't* enjoyed what he'd done—But no. There was no mistaking her satisfaction. Why had she cried then?

His reaction to the scent of her tears had been instantaneous, almost a physical pain. It provoked twin, seemingly opposing physiological responses in him. Hyper focus—his body alert, ready to shift to protect her from whatever danger, but also a calm, as if to enable him to properly soothe her. He tried to remember if he'd ever felt that with a female before. Had one ever cried near him? He feared this reaction was also particular to a mate.

He flipped the caps off the beers and carried them by their necks to the sofa.

Melissa turned up her nose and refused it.

"Sorry, I don't have any microbrews for you, princess."

She rolled her eyes, blushing as if it embarrassed her to be called out in front of Mark. That only made him want to stuff the wolf headfirst down his toilet.

Mark was in the middle of telling Melissa something—probably something he should've been listening to. "The dispensary where Jeremy works got knocked over a few nights ago. Jeremy was the one who reported it to the police."

Melissa nodded, as if she already knew this information.

"I'm guessing that he robbed it himself, or was in on the deal and that's why Rabago is after him."

Melissa paled.

"Do you know anything about it?"

She blinked rapidly, like she was holding back tears. "No," she said, her voice wobbly. "I think you must be right. He came home that night and told me about the holdup. I thought he'd seemed excited and had written it off to the adrenaline of the drama, but this makes more sense."

Mark nodded. "Who do you think he'd be working with?"

She swallowed, then shook her head. "I don't

know. Could be any one of his buddies. They're all shit-for-brains."

Cody didn't mind her bitterness toward Jeremy, but what bothered him was how much emotion the fuck-up elicited from her. Why was that? Did she still care about him, despite it all?

"And you haven't heard from Jeremy since yesterday? When did you see him last?"

"When I left for work in the morning."

"Did he go to work that day?"

"I don't know." She brushed a strand of her auburn hair from her face. The haunted dullness in her eyes made him want to wring her bastard ex-boyfriend's neck.

"And you've tried to contact him?"

"Yes, I texted him and warned him not to come home. He never responded."

"Well, I'd like to get my hands on him before Rabago does. We could offer him protection in exchange for testimony against the kingpin. Barring that, Ben has offered to pay Rabago whatever it is Jeremy owes him in order to get you free and clear of the threat. That's my second choice, though. I'd rather get this asshole off the streets."

Melissa's head wobbled as she nodded. "I don't want Ben to have to pay off Jeremy's debt, either."

"So what happens if Rabago finds Jeremy first?" Cody asked. Personally, he preferred the second option. The sooner Melissa was out of the line of fire, the better. Then he could be done with all this mess. Except that didn't feel right, either. He wasn't done exploring this physical attraction he had for her.

Yeah, he just needed to fuck her and get it out of his system.

"Then Jeremy's probably a dead man. But they'll want the money back before they kill him, so keeping Melissa safely off the grid would be even more important. If they catch Jeremy, they're going to torture him and they definitely would dangle the threat of Melissa's death over his head to get him to sing."

Melissa had gone pale. "You need to find Jeremy before he does, then." She stared at her hands, and some itchy instinct told him she might know where to find the guy.

"Right," Mark agreed.

"If Ben paid Rabago off, who would broker that deal?" he asked.

Mark's lips tightened to a thin line. "I don't know. It can't be me or anyone on my team. Ben would kill me if I let Melissa do it, although she's the most likely candidate."

"I'd kill you first," Cody muttered, drawing a raised brow from Melissa. "I could do it."

Mark tapped the tips of his fingers together, his elbows resting on his knees. "You're willing?"

"Yeah."

"You'd be my first choice, too. Mainly because I'd want it to be a wolf and I know you could handle yourself if something went wrong. Like I say, I'd rather we not go that route, though."

"Any idea where the stolen money might be?" Cody asked Melissa.

She shook her head. "None. We were hardly speaking the last few months and we never were that close."

His lip curled, but he bit back any questions about why she was living with some asshole she never liked. He'd save those for another time.

"You're okay keeping her here?" Mark asked. "If not, I can take her up to Denver and provide protection."

He bristled, even though his brain said he was way better off having her off his hands. "She'll stay here," he snapped.

Melissa frowned.

"I can provide adequate protection."

Mark turned a curious gaze on him. "I wasn't questioning your ability to provide protection," the agent said mildly.

"Right." He knew he sounded surly, but couldn't help himself. Everything seemed to piss him off when it came to Melissa.

"Well, locals are on the lookout for Jeremy. I'll send them over to Melissa's place to see if they can pick up Rabago or his guys for breaking and entering. That doesn't mean it's safe to return home, though," Mark warned Melissa.

She scowled, but nodded.

Mark stood up and he and Melissa both followed suit, shaking hands with him again and seeing him out.

When he left, Cody blew out his breath and put his hands on his hips. This whole thing was a cluster fuck.

MELISSA WATCHED Cody pace around his small living room. A muscle jumped in his jaw, his brows were down low. Even though she hadn't been the one to call in the favor, regret speared her for getting him involved.

"I don't want you to bring that money to Rabago," she spoke from the couch.

He whirled and glared at her. "Why not?"

"You shouldn't have to risk your life like that. This isn't your mess and you've already done enough to help me. I should bring it."

"Like hell," he growled.

"I'm sorry Ben dragged you into this. You don't even know me and it's not your stupid drama. I know this is more than you bargained for."

He raised an eyebrow. "Is it? I gave Stone an alpha's promise to protect you. That means my life for yours. So yeah. I already signed up for this." He continued to pace, his hands on his hips, nostrils flaring in anger.

She stood up and blocked his path. "What are you so pissed off about, then?"

He cursed and jabbed his fingers through his hair, sending it off in different directions. Holding up a finger, he said, "One, I can't figure out why you were with this douche in the first place."

She recoiled, bitterness filling her mouth. "Yeah, well, neither can I, okay?" Her voice had risen in pitch. "I have terrible taste in men, a problem which I soon plan to remedy." She threw a dark look his way, but flinched when he seemed to read her mind—that he was one of the men she planned to avoid.

He stepped up to her, toe to toe, glaring down. "What is that supposed to mean?"

She flushed but didn't back down. "It just means I'm done with losers. I'm going to find someone honorable. And stable. And normal."

And boring.

The muscle in Cody's jaw jumped again.

She folded her arms across her chest defiantly. "You said *one*. Was there more?" She didn't know why she was goading him, why she needed to have this fight, but she did.

"Yeah, there's more." He stopped pacing and

lifted his hand to gesticulate, but then seemed to stop himself. "Never mind," he growled.

"What the hell?" She was totally game for dragging everything out onto the table. "If you don't want me here, you shouldn't have told Mark I should stay with you. And by the way, one of you should have asked me what *I* prefer, don't you think?"

"What do you prefer, princess?" His words came out icy this time, instead of red hot and she registered the change with a bit of shock. Where was all this venom coming from? He pointed to the door. "You prefer Mark to be your protector? Is that it? It's okay for Ben to drag him into it, but not me? I guess he's got more of the knight in shining armor thing going with that suit and badge, doesn't he?"

She jerked as if he'd struck her, and understanding finally dawned. She'd offended his pride. Going soft and swearing he misunderstood wasn't going to put out this fire. She strode over to him and jabbed his chest with a finger.

"Fuck, no."

He glowered down at her, waiting.

It was hard to say more. They were always at odds with each other. She didn't like to give him an inch. But she didn't like him pissed off either. "You're the only knight in shining armor around here that I see."

He looked wary, like he thought she was blowing smoke up his ass.

"Mark's just doing his job. You're the one who offered me pack protection. If you weren't always such a smug, cocky bastard, I might have shown a little more gratitude."

The corners of his mouth twitched.

Her heart jumped around in her chest while she watched his gaze turn from scalding to smoldering —with a different kind of heat. "I don't need your thanks," he muttered and reached for her nape, yanking her in to claim her mouth, just as he'd done in the middle of the mall. She closed her eyes and melted into the kiss, which was no less violent or consuming than the last one.

One of his hands slid down her back and gripped her ass, squeezing and pulling her hips against him. He wedged one leg between her thighs, and her hips rocked down to rub her clit against it.

She moaned.

"That's it, baby, keep up that sexy moaning." He bit her ear, teeth grazed her jaw before he returned to fuck her mouth with his tongue.

She rolled her pelvis up and down on his thigh, the stimulation against her clit driving her mad.

He lowered and curled his forearm under her ass, lifting her easily to straddle his waist. She looped her arms around his neck, lips still twisting over his in a desperate dance.

She knew it was a bad idea. She didn't want to get into a relationship with another bad boy like Cody. But since the moment he'd first grabbed her in her bedroom closet, she'd been fighting the attraction. Maybe if she just let things ride, the tension would ease between them. It didn't mean she had to be in a relationship with him.

Cody lifted her higher and bit her breast. She shrieked. "Shirt off, Melissa."

Not a request. A command.

Could she handle this guy? He wasn't all human. Maybe the wolf part would be too much.

"*Now*," he gritted. "Or I'll tear it off."

She yanked the t-shirt off and threw it on the floor. Cody backed her against the wall and pinned her. He yanked down her bra.

"Ow," she protested when the strap dug into her shoulder. "What the fuck, Cody?"

Cody froze, panting, his eyes glinting ice blue. After a moment, the color faded to slate. He eased his grip and she slid down the wall to her feet.

Regret washed over his features. He cupped her face and brushed her cheek with his thumb. "Fuck, Melissa. I'm sorry. You're going to get hurt with me."

The dire prediction echoed the conclusion she'd already drawn, but that didn't make it any easier to hear.

Her clit throbbed in rhythm with her pounding

heart. The bra hung half off her, one strap still clinging to her shoulder. She hadn't wanted him to stop.

He stroked his hand up and down the side of her neck, following it to the slope of her shoulder. "Baby… I can't—" He blinked. "I shouldn't…" He shook his head. "Humans are too fragile for wolves. Believe me, there's nothing I want to do more than part those sexy thighs and fuck the ever-loving attitude out of you, but—" He leaned close and inhaled against her neck. "Your scent drives me fucking crazy and I just might lose control and bite you and neither one of us wants that."

She worked to swallow around the knot in her throat. "Right," she whispered hoarsely, although she wasn't quite sure what he was saying. Obviously, mating her would be a big mistake.

Okay, fine. She agreed.

She shoved at his chest and he stepped back. "It's late. I'm going to bed," she mumbled.

He didn't answer, which was probably just as well. They really didn't have much else to say to each other, did they?

7

Cody slept in wolf form. It seemed the safest idea—less temptation to go in the bedroom and finish what he'd started with the beautiful redhead sleeping there. He woke at dawn and nosed into the bedroom.

Melissa sat up, beautiful with her long, thick waves sleep-tousled, her cheeks flushed. His wolf almost whined at the sight of her. Her blue eyes widened at the sight of him, but she climbed out of bed and came toward him. She wore one of his t-shirts, and her long, bare, shapely legs would've made him groan if he was in human form.

He trotted toward the bathroom intent on shifting back in there, where she wouldn't see the gargantuan cock stand he got every time he shifted around her, but she stopped him.

"Cody?" Her voice was throaty from sleep.

He stopped and turned.

To his surprise, she buried her fingers in his fur. "May I pet you? Is this okay? I just wanted to feel…"

It took all his willpower not to shift back and tell her to touch the part of his anatomy that had been straining for her since the moment he first saw her.

She ran her hands over his body, stroking, petting.

It occurred to him that he hadn't been petted like that in years. Perhaps ever. No, his mom had pet his fur when he was a pup. But she'd been dead since he was eight, and his stepmother and father had never been very affectionate. And while he'd had sex, he hadn't had a girlfriend. Not someone who touched him just to feel. Not with any intent other than to stroke.

A shiver ran over his entire body. What was it? Pleasure? Not sexual pleasure, but something else.

She stroked his ears, buried her face in the fur of his neck.

He twisted and licked her shoulder.

She giggled, clinging more tightly.

He gave a shake and trotted away toward the bathroom, shifting just before he got there.

Melissa stopped short at the sight of his naked form, her mouth dropping open. When her eyes slid down to his jutting cock, he shrugged. "Happens when I shift."

He shut the door and turned on the water, ignoring the raging hard-on. He had to get to two worksites to check on progress, then meet with his agent. And he didn't like to leave Melissa alone for too long.

When he emerged from the shower, he found her in the living room, doing some kind of yoga routine on his floor.

He bit back a groan, his cock instantly hard again at the sight of her panty-clad ass sticking high in the air.

"Seriously, princess—are you trying to torture me?"

"I don't know what you're talking about," she said, a little too innocently. "I'm just practicing my downward dog."

If she was his mate, he'd hold her in that position while he fucked her into oblivion for teasing like that. The momentary fantasy of all the sexual games they'd play if they were mated glued his feet to the floor, his eyes still fixed on her oh-so-appealing ass.

And then he lost his hold on the tenuous control he had. Before he knew what he was doing, his feet crossed to her, hands peeled those panties down to her ankles.

She shrieked, laughing, and tried to twist away, but he looped a forearm under her waist to hold her in the position and smacked her ass.

She gasped. Nectar glossed her entrance, the scent of her arousal sending him into orbit.

He lifted his prisoner into the air and carried her to the sofa, where he sat down with her on his lap, her back against his front. "Put your hands on the floor."

"What?"

He didn't wait for her to obey, but maneuvered her himself, pushing her torso forward until her hands reached the floor and her legs straddled him, wheelbarrow style. "I'll show you my favorite yoga pose."

Her ass was presented to him, pussy spread and glistening.

"This isn't yoga," she protested, but he ignored her struggles, giving each cheek another perfunctory smack. She stilled.

He filled both hands with her ass, making small circles with his thumbs at the juncture of her inner thighs. "If you're a good girl, I'll get you off. Would you like that, baby?" He brushed her labia with his thumb and she made an indistinct mewl. "What's that?"

She didn't answer.

"Or did you need more spanking?" He slapped each cheek again smartly.

"No-o-o," she moaned. "I'll be good."

He brought his thumb to her dewy entrance and slid it slowly up and down, coating her vulva with her natural lubricant. "You want me to make you feel good, baby?"

"Yes," she breathed. "Cody…"

He really loved the sound of his name on her lips. "That's my good girl." He rubbed the pad of his thumb over her clit quickly, then slowed down for a few firm downward strokes.

"Ahh-ah," she cried out.

He gave her ass a light slap. "Settle down, beautiful. You don't come until I say you come, got it?" He had a feeling she'd go off like a firecracker with just a few strokes, and he intended to take his time. If he wasn't going to fuck the hot little human, he could at least savor the pleasure of bringing her to orgasm. He tossed a pillow down to his feet. "Make yourself comfortable."

She snatched it up and propped it on his feet, then rested her cheek on the pillow, arms wrapped around his legs.

He peppered her ass with several more spanks, loving the way her butt bobbed and arched for them, the way her inner thighs quivered and her pussy wept for his touch. "What happens to girls who tease?" He sank one thumb inside her while the rest of his hand cupped her mons and massaged her clit.

"Ahh!"

He slapped her ass with his other hand, delivering a sharp smack. "What happens?"

"This?" Her voice quavered.

He bit back a chuckle and slapped again in the same exact place, while still pumping his thumb in and out of her. "What is this?"

"Punishment," she gasped, humping his lap.

He removed his thumb and returned to focus on her clit, which had her squeezing the legs wrapped around his waist in a pulsing excitement.

He stopped and slapped her ass again. He dragged his thumb through her juices and brought them up to her anus, circling the little pink rosebud.

She scrambled, as if she wanted to crawl right off his lap. He caught her hips and yanked her back. "Where do you think you're going?" He pressed his thumb insistently at her rear entrance, waiting for the tight ring of muscles to relax.

His thumb breached her hole and he dropped some saliva on it to help lubricate, easing it in and out. He added his other thumb to her pussy and worked them alternately, pressing first one thumb in, then the other.

"Oh, my God," she wailed. "Cody…"

"Do you like your punishment, baby?"

"Yes," she breathed. "Please…"

"You want to come?"

"Yes, please. I'll be good."

A chuckle bubbled out of him, but he increased his speed and pushed both thumbs in at the same time, while the fingers of his lower hand pressed firmly against her clit.

She shrieked. "Cody! Oh Jesus, oh my God!"

"Come for me, baby."

Her scream echoed through his house, muscles clamped down on his thumbs. The unstrained pleasure on her face made a picture he etched forever in his mind as the most beautiful thing he'd ever witnessed.

When she collapsed over his lap and legs, fully spent, he bent to pull her back up, then swung her up into his arms and carried her into the bathroom. He stood her on her feet, but kept an arm wrapped snugly around her waist in case her legs wobbled. Passion had flushed her slack cheeks, and her glassy eyes were heavy-lidded.

He turned on the water and waited for it to warm up. When he tugged his shirt off her body, he nearly wept with need. Her apple-sized breasts pointed up, peach nipples forever optimistic. With a surge of lust, he gripped both her wrists and slammed them over her head to lift the impudent nipples even more. Her breasts lifted for his mouth, which he brought first to one, then the other.

The wolf within him surged and his vision domed. This time, he sensed the shift in his mouth, teeth lengthening, mating serum dripping.

No.

He used every bit of control he still had to pull

back and yanked the shower curtain open. "Get in." His guttural voice sounded like someone else's.

She stepped in, but gripped his shirt, pulling him toward the shower. "Cody... I'm sorry I got scared last night. You didn't hurt me. Let's try again."

The wolf raged at the surface.

Take her. Claim her. Make her yours.

His sharpened vision made her seem even closer. He stumbled back. "We can't," he grated harshly and he left the bathroom, and then the house, before the wolf could change his mind.

THE ORGASM HADN'T DIMINISHED her interest in Cody—not in the least. The way he'd taken her had been base and raw—utterly humiliating, and yet the orgasm he'd wrung had been out of this world. Which was why she'd been devastated when, yet again, he'd left her without a word. This time, though, she understood.

Cody wanted her. He wanted to mark her, even, like Ben had marked Ashley, only he apparently thought that would be a terrible idea. Tears stung her eyes.

She spent most of the day catching up on work. She posted photos of a new listing and put together the virtual tour. She called several clients to give them updates and put together comps for a house one of her clients was considering making an offer on.

Only after she'd done everything she needed to do, did she call Ashley for a heart to heart.

"So he won't have sex with me because he wants to mark me," she said dully.

"What? Oh, my God! Seriously? He thinks you're his mate?"

"No! That's the problem. He definitely doesn't want me as his mate. So it's a no-go. Which is fine, really, because he's a little too much my type, if you know what I mean."

Ashley paused. "No, actually, I don't. What are you trying to say?"

"Have you seen the guy? He looks like he could be a mob enforcer or a hitman or something. Covered in tattoos, works as a manual laborer."

Ashley was silent. "Did you just say *works as a manual laborer*?"

"I don't mean to sound snobby. I have nothing against blue collar work—obviously. I still work in a bar to make ends meet and every guy I've dated has had a menial job. It's just… I'd decided it was time for an upgrade. I want to date a normal, professional guy this time. Not some dark, dangerous, motorcycle-riding head of a wolf gang."

Ashley snorted with laughter. "I don't know, that sounds really hot to me. But I don't know if I called him a manual laborer. I mean, I thought Ben said he flips houses?"

"Yeah, he works for CJ Steele Construction, the company that refurbishes houses in the Old North End neighborhood—the ones I've been lusting after? But you know what I mean. He's not a doctor or lawyer."

"You're not even making sense. When did you ever want a doctor or lawyer?"

"That's the point!" she wailed. Usually Ashley understood her better than this. "It's not what I want, but it's what I should want. I'm done with bad boys and Cody is definitely a bad boy."

"Hmph," Ashley sniffed. "Well, I don't believe you, but it sounds like you need some time and space to figure out what you want next, and you're just getting out of a relationship, so don't rush. If Cody won't have sex with you, that's probably a good thing. You know you're way too loyal to people you've bonded with."

"Shut up."

"I'm not criticizing. It's what makes you an amazing friend and a perfect sister. It's what will make you the best girlfriend for the guy who doesn't take advantage of you."

"If that guy exists," she said sourly.

"He exists," Ashley murmured and Melissa heard the depth of her love for Ben. A pang of guilt over calling during their honeymoon made her forget her own dramas.

"Hey, get back to your groom. Your alpha wolf. Does he still bite you?"

Ashley laughed. "No, once he marked me he had more control."

"Good to know. Not that I'm going to be getting marked or anything. Have fun. Give him a killer blowjob today, okay?"

Ashley laughed. "He'll thank you for that suggestion. I'll talk to you soon. Love you."

"Love you, too," she said softly and hung up.

CODY CAME HOME that afternoon to find Melissa sitting on the couch with the Chromebook propped on her legs, looking adorably studious. He'd rushed through his tasks for the day, not wanting to leave her alone too long.

Or maybe it was the fact that her scent still lingered on his clothes, the vision of her, glorious and naked, trying to tug him into the shower that morning kept replaying in his mind until he could scarcely think.

She didn't look up immediately, but her cheeks colored, and he knew she was remembering what he'd done to her that morning. He smirked.

"Hey, baby. No special outfit to greet me today?"

She pursed her lips in what must be her attempt at prudish, but actually made her look even more sex-kitten. "That got me in trouble, if I recall."

He sauntered toward her, his cock already stiffening at the memory. "And I seem to recall you enjoyed your punishment. Quite a bit."

Her lips twitched, but she continued to play at ignoring him, clicking away on the computer.

The burner phone he'd bought her rang.

"I forwarded the calls from my old phone to this number," she explained as she picked it up. "This is Melissa." The blood drained from her face. "I don't know where he is," she croaked into the phone.

He rushed to her side and put his ear next to hers.

"You tell him Junior Rabago is looking for him, and I want my money back. He has until Friday to produce it."

"How much money does he owe you?"

"Fourteen grand, plus interest. I need it paid in full or you and your boy both die. Don't think I can't find you." He hung up.

Melissa drew a long, shaky breath. "Well… at least I know how to get a hold of him now, if we do use Ben's money to pay him off."

"We're paying him off. The sooner the better.

We need to get this guy off your back and out of your life."

"Do you think it will get him off Jeremy's back too?"

He glowered, hating that she mentioned the asshole. "Only if he's part of the delivery," he opined.

Her hand shook as she looked at the phone in her hand. "I talked to Ashley today and Ben said he could have the money transferred straight to your account, if you give him the routing and account number."

"I'll text it now." He moved away from her, no longer able to stay so close without shoving her onto her back and having his way with her.

She returned her focus to the Chromebook and her brow furrowed. "Oh, no!" she exclaimed, smacking her forehead. She tossed the Chromebook down on the sofa and jumped to her feet. "Oh crap, oh shit, crap shit crap!" She paced a rapid circle around his living room, shaking her fists in various directions.

"What? What is it?"

She whirled on him. "I forgot my little's birthday."

He stared at her. What in the hell was she freaking out about? "Your what?"

"My little. I'm in the Big Brothers, Big Sisters program. I was supposed to have a date with my little to celebrate her birthday last night. With everything that's going on, I totally forgot. She probably tried to call my phone but of course I don't have it—it's probably dead by now. I feel like such a schmuck."

He stared at her, surprised at how much she seemed to care about this. She'd just taken a phone call from a guy who'd threatened to kill her without freaking out, and *now* she was upset? Over a missed date with a charity case? Was the woman he'd pegged as superficial, if not selfish, actually this upset about an underprivileged kid? Just the fact that she participated in the program shocked the hell out of him.

"So tell her you'll make it up to her."

To his alarm, her big blue eyes swam with tears. "You don't understand. This is a totally underprivileged kid. Her mom's a stripper crack whore who barely keeps a roof over her head. She's probably never had a decent birthday in her life. I'd bought her a great gift and I—" She stopped, her chin wobbling.

"Baby." The need to comfort her made him want to howl. He wasn't any good at soothing women—he sorely lacked practice—but he sure as hell had to try. Tucking her against his side, he rubbed circles over her lower back. "Beautiful girl, don't cry. We'll go over there right now and explain. Well, we can't explain about people wanting you dead, but we'll tell her you had an emergency."

"But her gift," she moaned. "It's at my place."

"We'll get her a present on the way and you can tell her you have something else for her later. She'll get two birthdays. What kid wouldn't love that?"

Melissa sniffed. "You don't mind taking me there now?"

He cupped her chin and lifted her tearstained face. The sight of the moisture still tracking down her cheeks was unacceptable. He wanted to crush anything and everything that had ever made her cry. It unnerved him how much power her tears commanded over him. "As long as you stop crying," he muttered.

She gave a half-sob, half-laugh and shoved him away, dashing at the tears with the back of her hand.

They drove to Dairy Queen and picked up an Oreo ice cream cake, decorated with her little's name—Margot—because Melissa said she probably didn't get much with her name on it. With the cake on her lap and a Target gift card stuffed in her purse, Melissa sat rigidly beside him, shoulders square and stiff.

"How long have you been her big sister?" He wanted to know more about this side of Melissa. This unexpected and generous side.

"Not long." She raked her teeth across her

lower lip. "Six months. It's a project of Brown Realty. I didn't want to do it at first."

"Why not?" He expected her to say what a pain it was or to enumerate the problems with the program, but she stared out the window, still worrying her lip between her teeth.

"I get too attached," she said finally, with a sigh. "I don't do casual relationships. I'm all in and I never know when to quit."

Somehow he thought she might be talking about her ex-boyfriend, too.

She heaved another sigh. "I can't believe I missed her birthday date. I'm such a fuck-up."

His eyebrows shot up. That was his line. Did Melissa really see herself that way? If so, she'd been looking in the wrong mirror. "How are you a fuck-up?"

"Always have been," she said softly.

He hated the dullness in her voice, in her blank stare out the window. "I keep trying to better myself, but I just don't ever seem to get it right."

"I thought I said no more crying," he said, hoping to lighten the mood. It didn't work. She didn't even seem to hear him.

"Hey… I'm sure you're an amazing big sister. Margot's going to be thrilled."

"Ashley wouldn't have forgotten."

Ashley. Was that her twin?

"Melissa, you're being too hard on yourself."

"Ashley was the good twin. The one with perfect grades and high test scores. The one who got everything right."

His lip curled. He knew something about not measuring up to siblings. Quite a lot, in fact. "So what does that make you?"

She gave a harsh chuff of laughter. "I was the one cutting classes in high school. Trying drugs in the lower parking lot with the rough crowd. Dating assholes like Jeremy."

Ah. He hated that her asshole ex took up so much brain space for her, but at least she knew it had been a mistake.

He pulled up at the address for a low-income apartment building she'd given him and turned the truck off, twisting to face her. "Comparisons will fuck you every time, my friend," he said, trying to make his voice light. "Next to me, you were probably the golden child."

He watched her return to him then, blinking and losing the faraway stare. Her eyes searched his face with curiosity and it was his turn to sound bitter. "I have some perfect brothers, too. I hate the motherfuckers."

She laughed, sending relief flapping through his belly. "Yeah, I guess you're right." She shoved open her door and took the cake from her lap before they stepped out. The darted glance she sent from under her lashes seemed shy, as if she hadn't expected him to be a gentleman. Well, why in the hell should she? He'd practically gone out of his way to shock her with his basest manners.

They climbed the stairs—apparently there was no elevator in the place—to the third floor. The stained hallway walls and filthy laminate tile screamed volumes about the care the landlord took of the place. Yeah, he didn't keep his place spic and span, but that was because it was *his* and he didn't care. The houses he rented out or sold to others reflected the pride he took in restoring them, bringing them up to a higher code than people expected. That was what had made him successful.

Melissa knocked on one of the doors and shifted from foot to foot. He dropped a hand on her shoulder to reassure her. Seeing this vulnerable side of her brought out furious protective instincts. He wanted to repair every broken piece of her, sand down every surface of her life, to prevent her from ever getting another splinter.

And the urge terrified the shit out of him. Mad lust for her he at least understood. She was smoking hot, human or not. But this other instinct—the one that didn't seem to understand they weren't in a relationship, weren't attached in any way, didn't even like each other much—screamed *mate.* Screamed it even louder than the urge to mark her.

The door swung open and a lanky, sullen teen with blue-tipped hair that hung in her eyes peered out. She scowled at Melissa, although he thought he saw a glimmer of interest at the cake.

"Margot, I'm so sorry I missed our date. My house got broken into and I had to move out and… things just went haywire."

The girl stared over Melissa's shoulder at him. "Who's that?"

Melissa bit her lip. "This is Cody. He's, uh…" She darted an uncertain glance in his direction.

"I'm her bodyguard," he filled in. "Until we figure out who broke into her place and why." Stick close to the truth when dealing with humans. That's the way he'd always played it.

The teenager nodded, absorbing his position as if most people in her life walked around with beefy tattooed bodyguards. She looked down at the cake, then over her shoulder, where a television blared. A pair of feet hung off the edge of a ratty tartan couch. "You can't come in right now."

"That's okay. I just wanted to bring this over." Melissa handed her 'little sister' the cake, then took the gift card they'd picked up at the grocery store on the way over.

The teen switched the cake to one arm and reached for the gift card, finally cracking her first smile. "Thanks."

"Hopefully we can meet next week." She shot another glance at him. "But I'll let you know either way. I have a new number—I'll text it so you have it."

Margot narrowed her eyes. "Is everything okay?"

"Yes, I'll get it straightened out. I'm really sorry about yesterday." Melissa gave the girl an awkward hug.

Margot stiffened under the hug and ducked her head, so Melissa pulled quickly away. After an awkward goodbye, the door shut and he eyed Melissa, trying to get a read on how she thought it had gone.

She tilted her head up to meet his gaze. "Thanks."

Warmth seeped through his chest. It was just one word, but it shivered in the air between them, bare and exposed. She'd shown him her real self today—the one underneath the haughty exterior, and he didn't take the honor lightly.

He hooked an arm around her waist and started to pull her toward him, when a scent caught his notice. Whirling, his eyes came to rest on the female pup from the mall.

CODY HAD BEEN ABOUT to kiss her, but he stopped and turned. The girl they'd seen at the mall stood behind him, frozen, her green eyes wide.

"Hey." Cody's voice was kind—nothing like his usual gruff tones. "Where's your mom?"

The girl sucked her lower lip into her mouth and didn't answer.

"Will you tell her I'm here?"

Eyes still glued to Cody, she nodded and backed away from them, running to the end of the hall, where she pushed the last door open and disappeared inside.

Cody exchanged a look with her and set off down the hall, following. Melissa hurried to catch up, but then halted, wondering if she was intruding.

"Should I—? Maybe I'll wait down in the truck?"

Cody stopped and frowned. "Not safe." He held out his arm and when she arrived at his side, he tucked her in against him. It seemed so natural, she almost forgot how strange it was to have the tension between them eased. She knew she'd thrown him for a loop when she'd lost it back at his place, but forgetting Margot's birthday had been unforgivable. She'd worked for months just to get a rapport going with the girl, and to lose it all because she'd been so self-absorbed just killed her.

But Cody had been amazing. She really hadn't expected him to comfort her or even to take her dilemma seriously. She definitely hadn't expected him to help her fix things. Maybe she'd misjudged him.

They stood outside the apartment door, but Cody didn't knock. Instead he leaned a shoulder against the wall, keeping her nestled against his other side.

The door opened as far as the chain lock would allow and the pale, gaunt face of the shifter female peered out. Her gaze swiveled from Cody to her and back to Cody. Her nostrils flared and Melissa knew she must be scenting them.

"Lived here long?" Cody asked when she didn't speak.

She shook her head rapidly, causing her blond hair to fall in her eyes. "Just a few weeks. We're new to town."

Cody waited again, but she didn't elaborate. When he spoke again, he adopted a tone she hadn't heard from him before. It was slow, patient. Like he knew the female would spook if he showed too much aggression. "I'm Cody. This is my friend Melissa. We aren't here to hurt you."

The woman studied them both a moment longer, then, looking as if it was against her better judgement, slid the lock on the door and let it swing open. "Would you like to come in?" She sounded resigned, tired.

Melissa hid her shock as they stepped into the dingy apartment. There was no furniture in the tiny studio, save a single mattress with a quilt pulled over it. Both children sat on it, watching the newcomers.

"Are you the alpha?" the woman demanded. She sounded slightly bitter rather than submissive, but she didn't meet Cody's eye with any kind of challenge.

Cody nodded once and shoved his hands in his pockets. Melissa marveled at how much less intimidating it made him look. Rather than pulling the alpha domination bullshit he'd laid on her, he'd reeled it way in with this woman, which warmed Melissa to him even more. Based on her pinched, nervous expression, the woman was already afraid enough. She looked like a cornered animal. Which made her possibly dangerous, considering she had pups to protect.

"I'm not staying long," she bit out. "That's why I didn't come to see you." Her skin had a grayish, malnourished pallor and she was missing two teeth on the top.

Cody gave a nod, which could've meant anything. "Where are you from?"

Her shoulders rode closer to her ears. "Here and there."

"Name?"

The woman hesitated. "Colleen."

Cody pulled his hand out of his pocket and produced his wad of bills. Without unrolling them, he held them out to her. "Looks like you could use a little help getting on your feet, Colleen."

She didn't move to take the money. "I'm not

joining your pack." Though the words were bold, she kept her gaze lowered.

Without taking his gaze from her, he changed the angle of his hand to hold the money out to the children. The boy, who looked to be around ten, scampered forward without hesitation and took it.

Smart kid.

Cody produced a business card. The fact that he carried cards when he didn't even use a wallet surprised her, but maybe it was for pack business. He handed it to Colleen. "Our full moon run is tomorrow in the Woodland Park area, up Highway 24."

The children perked up, as if he had said they could go to an amusement park.

Cody smiled. "The pups are welcome, of course. There's a cabin there you can use any time. Call or text me if you want directions."

The woman took the card, uncertainty arresting her face. The children had risen from the bed and were crowding her, looking up with pleading expressions.

"Can we, Momma?" the girl asked.

Colleen's lips pressed together.

"You know how to reach me now." Cody's words both acknowledged she hadn't reached out to him and let her off the hook. He pointed to the card. "Use it if you need it."

Her expression shuttered, but she tucked the

card in the back pocket of her baggy jeans. "I appreciate you stopping by." She stared at the floor as she delivered this nicety, which sounded like utter bologna.

Cody sauntered toward the door, then looked back at the children, who had been watching him avidly, and now lowered their gazes to match their mother's. "I hope to see you Sunday. The mountain is beautiful."

No one answered, but Cody had already opened the door, as if he hadn't expected one. He let Melissa go first, his hand lightly resting at her lower back. So the guy did know how to be a gentleman, despite his Neanderthal act.

When they climbed in the truck, she said, "That was nice of you."

Cody stared at the steering wheel, looking grave. "Haven't had to deal with anything like that before."

"Like what?" She spoke softly, not wanting to knock him out of this uncharacteristic openness.

"Domestic abuse. I'm guessing she's hiding from whoever knocked those teeth out."

Melissa flinched to hear it spoken out loud, but she knew immediately Cody must be right. She studied his face, seeing him through a different filter. Cody as alpha—not just the guy who asserted his dominance sexually, but the one in charge of his pack. He seemed terribly capable. Dangerous, but not in the bad boy way, more in the protective way.

"You can… you'll protect her, right?"

His beautiful gray eyes stared back at hers, expression inscrutable. Shit. Maybe she shouldn't have asked about pack business. But jeez. She hoped he would help that woman. He rubbed his face. "If she asks for my protection, it's hers. You'll notice she didn't ask. She might be afraid she can't trust me—that I'll rat her out to her mate, whoever the abusive asshole might be, or she might not think I have enough power behind me to protect her."

He started the truck and pulled away from the curb. "You shouldn't look at me like that."

"Like what?"

"Like I'm a fucking hero. Because I'm not. And I like that look on you too damn much."

Her breath hitched. Cody wasn't looking at her, but the energy between them sparked.

He was a hero, though. He'd signed up to put his life before hers, without ever having seen her. And now he was ready to protect this other woman, who he didn't even know.

Unable to think of anything to say, she kept her mouth shut, ignoring the buzzing traveling through her body just at the nearness of Cody.

8

Cody parked the Ducati Streetfighter in front of his mountain cabin. Considering he had Melissa with him, he should have driven to Woodland Park in the truck, but the day was too beautiful. The open air ride through the mountain pass of Highway 24 was glorious, especially because he could bypass the jam-up of cars on the bike.

Choosing to ride the Ducati had nothing to do with the pleasure of having a certain beautiful redhead's thighs straddling his hips, arms around his waist. Nor had it been about shoving his hellion ways in her face again. Right.

It *might* have had something to do with not thinking himself capable of sharing the cab of the truck with her for the trip, inhaling her scent and suffering through small talk. He wouldn't have lasted ten minutes without giving into the need to shove the seat back and tell her where he'd like her mouth to go. Especially with the moon full and his beast so close to the surface.

Melissa unclasped her hands from their hold around his waist. He immediately missed having her body notched against his back. He expected her to look annoyed about having her hair mussed or the trip being too frightening—she'd held him in a death grip the entire time—but she wore a smile when she pulled off the helmet. When she gave her auburn waves a toss, sending them cascading over her slender shoulders, he distinctly heard the *chicka-bow-wow* play in the background of his mind.

Her eyes weren't on him, though. She walked toward the cabin with eagerness plastered all over her face. "Wow. When you said cabin, I wasn't picturing a full-on mountain retreat."

One corner of his lips kicked up at her girlish enthusiasm. He hadn't been prepared for this reaction. She skipped up the steps while he unloaded the food from the saddlebags. "When was this built?"

"I finished it last year."

She whirled, her mouth open, her full lips forming a little *O*. "You built this? Yourself?"

He tried to ignore the cascade of pride her awe provoked. "Yeah." He reached past her and hit the code on the security pad to unlock the door, somehow managing not to shove her against it and press his ever-eager cock against her lush, jean-clad ass.

"Oh, my God," she breathed, rushing in the moment he pushed open the door. "This is so beautiful." Her gaze swept over the oversized living room as she charged forward, checking out all the rooms. "I love the vaulted ceilings and the blend of rustic with high-tech. It's just like a CJ Steele home. This is incredible. What's the square footage, three thousand?"

"Thirty-two hundred." He didn't mean to, but he dropped the saddlebags with their clothes and food and followed Melissa as she rushed through the cabin.

"Four bedroom, two bath?"

"That's right."

"And this? Where did you find these carved supports?"

"I carved them." His throat tightened. He wasn't sure why he cared so much what she thought of the place.

"Who made this sink? It's incredible."

The sink was a hand-thrown and fired clay pottery beauty in shades of ochre and rust. "A friend of mine makes those."

"Does Mr. Steele use these in any of his houses?"

A shard of irritation jabbed him. Her hero worship of 'Mr. Steele' was so at odds with her condescension toward him. Some stubborn part of him needed her to respect *him*, the guy standing in front of her, not the real estate success she worshipped.

"Yeah, these sinks are in a few of his properties."

"Cody." She turned.

He fucking loved hearing his name on her lips, although he loved it more when she was screaming it at the height of a climax. He schooled his features, hoping to hide the dirty thoughts looping through his mind on a constant playback. "Yeah?"

"Do you own this place?"

"It belongs to the pack." That wasn't exactly an untruth. He'd built the cabin for the pack—a meeting place and a getaway for anyone who needed it. It had taken him four years, working weekends, but he'd loved every minute of it. Nearly every member of the pack had contributed their labor for it, too, which made it truly fitting as their home base.

"This property is worth a lot." The awe in her voice should not please him so damn much. He didn't want to impress her with money, after all.

"How much would you list it for?" He was curious about her skill as an agent. She said she'd lost a deal with him. Had she improved since then?

"Four ninety-eight for a quick sale. Five thirty if you wanted the perfect buyer."

"The perfect buyer? Who is that, exactly?"

"It's the person who will love your property as much as you do. The one who will take care of it, or improve it. The one who will give it a new story."

He stared at her, fascinated. His agent sure as hell never talked about people loving his properties. There was no emotion discussed in any of his transactions. Yet, watching her face light up as she described this love for a property, he knew exactly what she meant. He loved every property he ever worked on. And it was, sometimes, hard to turn his back on them when he sold. He'd never considered finding the 'right' buyer as a means of easing that pain.

"How would you show me this property, if I were a client?"

One corner of her lips lifted and her eyelids drooped slightly, as if talking real estate was a form of foreplay for her. She returned to the front door and beckoned him over. He pictured her in the tight skirt and heels she'd been wearing on the day he met her, her long auburn waves done up in a French twist. No—scratch that—hair down for this fantasy, always hair down, tempting his fingers to wrap it in his fist and pull. He sauntered to her side.

"I think you're going to be blown away by this place, Mr.—er—" She stopped, eyes seeking his face for help with her pretend game.

He didn't want to tell her his last name was Steele. Not now, maybe not ever. "Cody."

She rolled her eyes but went on. "Mr. Cody. It's more a work of art than a mere building. One of the members of the CJ Steele Construction team built this one, and it has all the same touches, which raises its value significantly. In time, I believe CJ Steele properties will become as sought after as, say, Frank Lloyd Wright buildings in other cities."

Cody gaped at her. Was she really comparing him with an architect? An artist? Some unknown emotion threatened to expand his chest beyond comfort. An itchiness came over him, like he needed to shift and run. But from what, he wasn't sure. Maybe from the feelings closing his throat.

She stepped to the center of the room and pointed toward the floor. "The wood floor looks like pine, but it's actually Australian cypress"—she shot him a questioning look and he nodded in affirmation—"which is a harder wood and far more durable. Notice the builder chose to leave the interior walls as the same rough log as the exterior. This is a classic CJ Steele technique of exposing the raw materials. He doesn't hide anything; instead he puts it front and center. In his industrial remodels, he exposes brick and uses the steel housing for electrical wires as a focal point. Here, in this cabin, he brings the outdoors in, yet still provides every comfort you'd crave in a getaway." She trailed off with her monologue and looked at him sheepishly. "I know it's not really a CJ Steele house, but I would sell it that way. Maybe I'd be cheating the buyer, I don't know." She shrugged.

He tried to speak around the knot in his throat. When nothing came out, he pulled her against him and crushed his lips to hers.

She gasped, jerking in surprise, then softening into the kiss. He slid his tongue between her lips, holding her nape to keep her captive. Then, because the little control he had was slipping, he pulled away.

"So your royal highness can stand the digs while I run?" He didn't know why he had to poke her with that again, when he liked her the way she was now, soft and appreciative. It probably had something to do with needing something to wedge between them, because as much as his inner wolf screamed she was his, he didn't want her. Not a human. He wasn't going to make his father right.

She flinched, and when she turned, the haughty tilt of her chin told him his barb had hit its mark. "Is this just a new cage to lock me in while you go off and do your thing?" She put her hands on hips, her perky breasts seeming to taunt him through her snug cotton tee. "Am I allowed to step out the door?"

Hating the way he'd changed things between them, he picked up the saddlebags and tossed the food supplies in the refrigerator. "You're safe enough here. You can sit outside on the deck, but don't go further than that."

She sniffed. "I should've brought the Chromebook up here."

"There's no Wi-Fi or cell phone signal. We're out of range."

"So exactly what do you think I'm going to do while you're off on your run?"

"You could make yourself useful and get dinner ready for the pack." He didn't mean it, but he knew it would annoy her.

Her eyes narrowed. "Great, so the wolves go on a run and the lowly human stays home to cook their meal? This patriarchal wolf dominance thing is starting to get old."

"You love the way I dominate you." He stalked closer to her, backing her into a wall.

Her breath hitched, eyes dilated.

He sank his fingers into her hair and massaged her scalp before he tugged her head back.

"Ow. What are you doing?"

The scent of her arousal made him insinuate his knee between her legs before the thought even entered his brain. "Princess, the moon is full. Leaving you here and going for a run isn't a pleasure, it's a necessity. You want to know why?"

Her plump lips parted. "Yeah."

"Because, baby." He grazed her ear with his

teeth. "If I spend one more second in here with you, I'm going to tear your clothes off and fuck you so long and hard you won't be able to ride that motorcycle back tomorrow."

She licked her lips and his eyes tracked the movement with hunger.

"Don't tempt me like that, princess. You know I'd love to shove my cock in that hot little mouth of yours."

He'd finally gone too far. Melissa shoved him back. "Jesus, Cody."

He pulled his shirt off and her eyes widened, dipping to his chest and abs, following his happy trail to the place it descended into his jeans. He laughed darkly as he walked to the bedroom, unbuttoning his jeans. He kicked them off and shifted, running for the dog door at the rear before his paws hit the wooden floor.

Melissa's heart pounded for long moments after Cody disappeared. Her panties were soaked, a constant every time she was around that dominant, dirty-talking wolf. Just once, she'd like to put him in his place, or send him off-kilter the way he always made her feel.

She looked around the place, wavering between self-pity over Cody dumping her there without much explanation about what was happening with the pack and their run, and pleasure at the incredible surroundings. The cabin—if you called it that—blew her mind. It was odd Cody didn't realize how impressive it was, but then, he worked on CJ Steele projects all the time. Still, he owned this property—or his pack did. And she would put its value at close to a half million if it included as much land as she suspected it did. This property combined with the one he owned in the Old North End neighborhood put him at a net worth far higher than she'd originally estimated. Cody wasn't just some construction worker living paycheck to paycheck. Or if he was, he'd invested wisely. She'd definitely misjudged him.

She thrust the pang of guilt away. He may have financial resources, but that still didn't make him dependable. Or nice.

But nice didn't go as far as she wished it did for her where it came to men. Never had.

Cody's brand of 'not nice' was about as sexy as it came. And while he may lack manners and have a degrading treatment of women, he wasn't doing anything illegal, like Jeremy. He earned an honest living. Had a decent amount of honor, actually.

She gave the property another thorough inspection, admiring the beautiful craftsmanship. There wasn't one thing she would change if she bought the place. Not one request she would have made differently had the house been built for her.

She sighed. Soon, hopefully a CJ Steele house would come on the market and Ben would help her buy it.

An hour passed and Cody hadn't returned. She went through a pair of French doors outside to the porch. The back of the cabin faced an expanse of woods. To the right, the mountain climbed upward, lichen-covered boulders dotting the wooded slope. A path led around the base of the incline, beckoning to her. No other building or property appeared in any direction from the cabin.

She drew in a deep breath of the crisp mountain air, rich with the scent of pine. The forest looked so welcoming. If Rabago and his cronies hadn't found her at Cody's place in Colorado Springs, they sure as hell wouldn't find her here. Pulling on her jacket, she jogged down the porch steps. She wanted to know where the path led.

She followed it a half mile until it stopped at what appeared to be a natural spring bubbling up from the earth. Someone had fashioned a pebble-bottomed pool and fit a copper pipe at the mouth. A tin cup lay nearby. She picked it up and filled it with water, then drank. Cold as ice and incredibly refreshing. She closed her eyes, savoring the treat.

A low growl startled her. Two huge tan wolves

closed in on her, fangs bared. The cup clattered to the rocks and she swallowed a shriek.

"Uh… easy…" She took a step back and the two wolves crept forward, teeth gleaming in the afternoon light.

Were they shifters? They must be; they were gigantic. Female shifters.

"I'm with Cody?" It sounded more like a question. She wasn't sure how much shifters understood when in wolf form. "Easy, girls. I-I'm not infringing on your territory or anything." Too late, she remembered to drop her eyes and not challenge them.

A movement to her left drew her eyes and she saw three more giant wolves, two black and one tan, watching. They were males. Was this some kind of mating thing?

She held her open palms out. "I'm not a threat, guys."

One of the female wolves snarled and leapt forward, jaws snapping an inch from where her hand had been before she jerked it back. She stumbled into the spring, back against the rock. Her sneakers soaked through with the freezing cold spring water.

Another snarl came from behind her and silver fur flashed over her head. She screamed as a wolf flew from the rock above her and knocked down the snapping female. The silver wolf took the tan one to the ground and rolled with it, throat between its jaws.

Cody? Yes, his huge, magnificent wolf form was unmistakable.

A horrible, pitiful yelp echoed off the rocks and the female rolled to her back, showing her belly. For one horrible moment, Melissa thought the silver wolf had killed the tan one, but when he pulled back, there was no blood at her throat. He nipped her hindquarters and she lay still, whining.

The other tan wolf had dropped to her belly and now crept forward, also whining. He growled and nipped her as well, then turned and trotted away, in the direction of the cabin. All the wolves fell in behind him, tails tucked as they followed.

Melissa stood frozen for several long moments, willing her heart rate to return to normal. The discomfort of the ice-cold water soaking her shoes finally forced her out of her stupor. She walked on shaky legs back to the cabin. When she pushed open the front door, she found young people had filled the large living area, and more were coming out of the bedrooms in various states of dress.

Two young women stood talking as one pulled on her socks and shoes. The other, a wiry woman with a pierced lip pulled her sandy blond hair into a ponytail. When she saw Melissa, her conversation died on her lips.

Cody stalked from the master bedroom wearing

nothing but his faded jeans. His feet were bare, as was his torso and her mouth went dry at the sight of his washboard abs and muscled chest. He wasn't paying any attention to her, though. The pissed-off wolf stalked over to the blonde. "You don't ever attack a female under my protection, whether she's wolf or human," Cody snarled.

Melissa's heart took off at a gallop again. Of course this had been the female who had attacked her.

"We didn't know she was with you," the woman said with fake innocence.

"Bullshit. My scent is all over her and you know it." He put his barrel chest in front of the girl and stared her down, the muscle in his jaw flexing.

"Sorry, Alpha." The she-wolf dropped her eyes but her tone didn't sound sincere.

The rest of the young people had gathered and stood watching the scene. Cody whirled on them. "What about the rest of you—standing around watching out there? What in the hell is wrong with you?"

The young men lowered their eyes and muttered things like, "Sorry, man," or "Sorry, Alpha."

"Well, why did you bring a human here?" the blonde challenged. "Is this your… *girlfriend* or something?" She said *girlfriend* like the idea disgusted her.

Finally, Cody glanced Melissa's way. "This is

Melissa. She's Ben Stone's sister-in-law. Ben requested pack protection for her and I gave it."

Of course she hadn't expected him to claim her as his girlfriend, but his words sliced through her nonetheless. Right, she was an obligation he had to Ben. The glow of satisfaction she'd had at his defense of her died a quick death.

"So she's allowed to just run out on our mountain during full moon?"

The low growl from Cody was pure animal.

The girl held up her hands, looked away and offered her throat. "I'm just asking."

"She's under our protection," he repeated firmly, but then shot Melissa a condemning look.

Damn. She hadn't realized she would be causing such a problem with the pack.

Cody turned around the semi-circle, but no one met his gaze. "If anyone fucks with her again, I'll put you in your place, and you will not like it. Do you hear me?"

"I liked it last time." The blonde gave Melissa a little smirk.

The blood drained from Melissa's face and her gut twisted. She'd been so thrown by the wolf dynamics she'd missed the obvious—this girl was Cody's lover. Or ex-lover.

Melissa had no right to the jealousy burning in her gut, but she seriously wanted to punch the woman. Of course, she'd be sure to lose any fight with a shifter, which only made her more furious.

"Get out." He pointed toward the door.

The blonde held up her palms. "Sorry. I was just joking. *Jeez.*"

He stared her down until all traces of the smirk faded from her face and a flush started up her neck.

"Sorry, Alpha."

A frown marring his handsome face, Cody surveyed the others in the room. "Anyone else have a problem we need to work out?"

A quick chorus of "No, Alpha" rang out.

"Good. Let's eat." Cody turned on his heel and walked to the kitchen.

Damn. She should not find it so hot to see Cody flex his wolf dominance with his pack, but she did.

Still, it was obvious she didn't belong here. She'd been clearly marginalized by Cody and the pack and Cody was obviously irritated with her for leaving the cabin. And she hated that she-wolf who'd just made her feel so stupid.

Unable to pull her face together, she slipped into the master bedroom and shut the door.

CODY STALKED out to light the grill, scowling at Lorna. As if it wasn't enough just to keep the beast in check around Melissa on the full moon, now he had some crazy pack drama playing out. His pack never had drama.

The group had fallen together easily. They were all in their twenties and he'd been the obvious leader. He'd never had to assert himself with them except in a joking manner. Most of them worked for him with CJ Steele Construction, and they had an easy relationship, with his employees working hard to please him, but knowing he wouldn't be a hard-ass if they needed slack.

Lorna's reaction to Melissa had taken him by surprise. He hadn't had sex with the she-wolf in over a year and they'd never been a couple—it had been gratuitous fucking, usually on a full moon, which is common among wolves until they find their true mate.

He should have warned the pack Melissa would be here. He'd told Greg, his beta, about the alpha promise, and had planned to tell the rest of the pack tonight, since it affected them all. But he wasn't thinking clearly, hadn't been since the night he brought Melissa home. She did that to him.

Voices picked up in the kitchen as the tension eased and the group fell into making food together. Greg, the beta of the pack, opened a couple of bags of chips and pulled a twelve-pack of beer from the refrigerator. Mary unwrapped a salad she'd brought.

He stepped in to get the meat, but something

made him freeze. Somehow, the scent of Melissa's tears had reached his senses. Where was she?

Dammit. The need to soothe her overrode any pack responsibility. Without a word to anyone, he stalked to the master bedroom and pushed the door open.

Melissa stood at the window, looking out. He caught her reflection in the windowpane, and the lost look nearly killed him. At his entrance, she whirled and darted away from him, into the bathroom.

He leaped forward, shoving his shoulder between the door and the frame before she could slam it shut.

"Can't I just get a little privacy around here?" She wrestled with him, trying to shove him out. He caught her wrists and twirled her to wrap her arms around her chest in a painless restraint, pulling her back against his chest and holding her tight.

"Hey," he said softly, trying to soothe her.

"Leave me alone."

He pushed her up against the wall, sandwiching her there between it and his body, his arms protecting her from being squished. She leaned her forehead against the wall, panting. He leaned his cheek against the back of her head, breathing in her scent.

He didn't know why she was crying—not exactly. And he wasn't good at handling distraught women—he'd had zero practice. But his instincts demanded he comfort her.

"Are you here to yell at me?" Bitterness threaded her voice.

"No, baby." Her heartbeat tapped through her back and into his chest. Her nearness both calmed and incited his beast.

"Why are you crying? Are you jealous because of what Lorna said?"

Her little body turned wiry against him, muscles tightening in reaction to his words.

He bit her ear, then laved it to soothe the sting. "You are, aren't you?" Pleasure swam through him. Good. He was glad she was jealous. If she had any idea the level of desire she inspired in him, she'd know he would tear the head off any man who looked at her twice.

"Go to hell."

"Baby, that she-wolf means nothing to me. I've full-moon fucked her a few times over the past few years, and that's it. It didn't mean anything and we've never been a couple." He wasn't sure why he needed to explain it to her—they weren't in a relationship either, nor did they want to be, but it seemed important she know how things lay.

He turned her in his arms to face him. "I'm sorry she was such a bitch to you. I didn't mean for that to happen."

Her lower lip trembled and it killed him to see her pain. "How many times?"

"What?"

"How many times is a few?" Then she shook her head. "Never mind. It's none of my business." She tried to shove him again. "Will you just go away?"

But it was her business. Her jealousy meant she had feelings for him, and despite his desire to stay emotionally clear of her, he cared about her, too. He wanted to ease her pain over this. He caught her chin and lifted it, brows knitting as he studied her beautiful face. "She never inspired one-tenth of the hunger I have for you. She never had me this tightly strung, seconds away from losing control every time I got close to her." He pressed his bulging erection against her belly. "Feel what you do to me. You think you need to be jealous over her?" He shook his head. "There's no comparison."

Tears swam in Melissa's eyes, but they didn't fall.

Soft and romantic wasn't his thing, but he did his best, tipping his head down to just brush his lips lightly across hers. "I'm sorry. That was a horrible introduction to the pack. Will you please come out and meet them now? The rest are nice and I will boot Lorna in a heartbeat if she's rude to you again."

She rubbed her lips together and nodded. "Okay."

Some of his tension eased. He twined his fingers into hers and led her out to the kitchen where at least ten members of his pack had now gathered. "Say hi to Melissa, everyone. She's a quarter wolf."

Their interest piqued at that, and Mary, the only other female in their little pack, drew Melissa over. Melissa complimented her salad and soon had her chatting nonstop about which ingredients she'd bought at the farmer's market.

By sunset, all twenty-five members of his pack had arrived and the noise in the cabin grew to a dull roar as they mingled and ate in casual potluck style. He considered asking Melissa to shut herself in the bedroom for the meeting, but decided against it. She'd already been marginalized enough and he wasn't worried about her sharing their secrets. If she did, he could take it up with Ben Stone.

9

Melissa watched as Cody emerged from the shower in the master suite, hair wet and tousled, the faded jeans and black t-shirt back on. Her pulse sped at the sight of him, so masculine and powerful.

It had been fascinating to watch him lead the pack meeting. He filled them in on Colleen and her kids and told them he'd protect her if she asked for it. His pack seemed less than enthusiastic, pointing out they knew nothing about her, and the very good possibility of a much larger pack coming for her. Cody listened to their feedback, thanked each member who spoke, but maintained his decision, unless something new came to light. He also filled them in on the details of Melissa's situation and the pack protection she required. No one spoke against it—probably still remembering Cody's anger earlier

—but from the dark looks many cast her, she under-stood protecting her wasn't popular either.

After the pack meeting, the wolves had gone back out to run again. It was midnight now and Cody had only just returned a few minutes before. He hadn't glanced her way when he entered—in wolf form—nor did he glance her way now as he padded out of the room.

She'd tried to sleep, but the eerie sound of the wolves howling outside made it impossible. That and the thought of her punishment. So she'd been standing at the window in one of Cody's t-shirts and the panties he'd bought her at Walmart, staring out at nothing for the last hour.

Cody returned to the room, holding a coil of rope, which he dropped on the beautifully carved rustic dresser before turning and leaning against it.

"Come here." There was dark promise in his look.

A shiver ran up her spine when she guessed what the rope was for.

Her pussy clenched. "Am I in trouble?" her words sounded smoky.

"Definitely." He crooked a finger at her.

She stepped forward. She trusted him, espe-cially after what happened in the bathroom.

In a swift movement, he picked her up by the waist and plunked her down on the dresser, inserting his body between her legs. He traced his thumb over her lower lip. His eyes were dark. "You disobeyed me today."

"I'm sorry. I didn't realize how much trouble it would cause for you." She attempted to speak around the tight band closing her throat. "I just wanted a little fresh air and I didn't think there was any danger of Rabago finding me here."

He leaned his forehead against hers. "It offended the pack to find you on their private grounds. I should have explained that to you. I should have thought to bring you something to do and I should have warned the pack you were coming. I'm sorry."

She drew in a breath, surprised at the apology. "Does that mean you're not going to… um, exert your wolf dominance on me?"

The corners of his lips lifted. "Sorry, baby. I never promise a consequence without delivering." He brushed a strand of hair back from her face, then burrowed his fingers into her thick mane, massaging her scalp.

She bit back a moan. God, she needed his touch. It seemed like the full moon affected her, too.

"Do you remember what I said would happen if you disobeyed me again?"

Yes. She remembered. "You said if I left the other house."

He gripped her hair and tugged her head back, causing her to cry out, though it didn't hurt that much. "How am I going to punish you, princess?" he growled.

She pressed her lips closed, refusing to answer.

His free hand came to grip her right breast and he leaned forward and bit her neck. "Say it," he whispered. He had a particular talent for turning almost any moment between them sexual. As always, her body responded, nipples beading up, heat flaring in her core.

"A—" She cleared her froggy throat. "A spanking."

"That's right," he purred, tongue flicking her earlobe. To her intense disappointment, he released her and stepped back. "Take off your clothes."

She slid off the dresser and held his gaze as she pulled his soft oversized shirt over her head.

The low growling sound in his throat was all about her bare breasts, which he stared at with a hunger that renewed her confidence. He snaked one arm around her waist and yanked her against his body at the same time he pinched one of her nipples between his fingers, hard.

She gasped in pain and surprise.

"Okay, princess. I'll make you a deal. If you bend over quietly and hold your position like a good girl, I will go easy on you."

"And if I don't?" she croaked.

His jean-clad cock pressed against her belly, hard and thick. He slid his hand down from her waist to her ass and squeezed. "If you can't hold still, then I'm going to tie you up with that rope over there. Because if I have to wrestle you, I will lose all control. You'll end up with my cock buried between your legs and my teeth in your shoulder. Then you'd be stuck submitting to an alpha wolf for the rest of your life, and I don't think either of us wants that."

The pleasure of his intense desire died with his last words.

He didn't want to be mated to her.

Of course he didn't. He didn't love her. She was just a stuck-up, pain-in-the-ass human to him. They may have a physical attraction, but it ended there.

She shoved at his chest. "I would never let that happen."

Cody grabbed her wrists and spun her around, holding them in the small of her back. "Rope it is." Was there a tinge of glee in his voice?

A shiver ran down her spine.

He wound the rope around her wrists behind her, then led her to the bed. "Bend over, princess." He smacked her ass.

She didn't immediately obey, but he didn't push her, maybe waiting for the consent implicit with her taking the position. She bent over and presented her ass to him.

With one hand pinning her in place, he took her panties down and delivered a couple sharp spanks.

It stung, but the sound of his groan distracted her. He sounded like he was in pain.

Good. It served him right. Let him suffer over the girl he didn't want to mate but couldn't keep his hands off.

He brought both hands to her ass and massaged her cheeks roughly, squeezing and opening her ass, then sliding his calloused palms down the backs of her legs and taking her panties off her ankles.

She moaned.

"Move and I'll double your punishment." His voice was smoke and velvet.

Her bottom clenched. She wanted more but also didn't want to keep fighting him.

"Good girl." With a stunning show of strength, he lifted her by the waist until she was on her knees on the bed. "I think I need you arranged a little differently." He returned with the rope and tugged her left ankle wide, then secured it to the bedpost.

"What are you doing?"

He didn't answer, but moved to her right leg, stretching it in the opposite direction and wrapping her ankle with tight coils of rope so that she lay on her belly with her legs spread-eagled.

"This is supposed to keep me safe?" she blustered. "You've just made it easy to do anything you want to me."

As if to underscore her fear, she saw his eyes

had turned pale blue as he stared at her with bald hunger.

"Shouldn't you be the one tied up?"

"That's not how it works." His voice had deepened and the bulge in his pants revealed his intense interest. "I'm the dominant wolf, princess."

BUT SHE WAS PROBABLY RIGHT. His vision had domed at the sight of her lying in such a provocative position, the pink heart of her sex exposed and spread wide, her juicy ass on display for his punishment. Lust rolled through in waves, making him dizzy.

But no. He had self-control. It was one of the many things he'd learned in the years since his father kicked him out of the pack. Drawing a deep breath, he rested one knee on the bed to get close enough and brought his hand down on one side of Melissa's ass.

The sound she made was pure sex.

He delivered three sharp slaps.

She gasped and the muscles in her back stood out in cords. Beautiful. She was fucking gorgeous.

He spanked her some more, loving the way she clenched her cheeks together and squirmed over the pillows; but he'd tied her without any slack, so she went nowhere.

He stopped and rubbed her ass. "Good girl." He continued, squeezing roughly, his lids going heavy with the pleasure of owning her sweet little ass.

She moaned. The scent of her arousal hit him like a drug, sending a wash of heat over his entire body. When she lifted her ass for more, he had to suck in his breath to keep from claiming her.

He wasn't about to untie her, not when the sight of her fulfilled every erotic dream he'd ever had. He slapped her pussy.

"Cody," she cried.

He slapped her pussy again, loving the wet kiss of moisture that came away on his fingers. Her arousal fueled his lust close to the breaking point.

He spanked down the inside of her left leg.

"Cody... Cody, please."

He fucking loved it when she begged.

"What do you need, baby?" He slapped her pussy with the belt again.

She wriggled her upper body, the only part of her able to move. "Oh, my God, Cody, please."

"Tell me." He spanked her pussy again.

"You! I need you... inside me."

The wolf in him roared and his vision domed. His jeans were down and off before he'd even taken a breath. Somehow, through the fog, he remembered to grab a condom from the bedside table.

Rip. Roll.

In the next second he'd buried himself, balls deep, without a thought to preparing her.

She gasped, her muscles tightening around him.

"Christ, did you just come?" His choked voice sounded far away.

"Yes," she panted. "I'm good. Go on."

He didn't need any encouragement. With a surge, he rocked back and in. Her fucktastic ass was hot and soft underneath him, her channel so deliciously tight, wet, and warm.

She made the cutest little grunts every time he plowed into her, but they were pushing him over the edge.

He reached around and covered her mouth with his palm. "Hush, baby. Stop making those sweet little sounds or I will come unglued."

She tongued his palm.

His teeth elongated.

No.

He lifted his head back and twisted his neck to turn it away from her, squeezing his eyes shut. "Don't move," he panted. "Don't make a fucking sound… I just need… to finish." But sliding in and out of her was too much. Her scent surrounded him, engulfed him. He roared, leaning on his knuckles beside her head, pounding his hips against her ass, hard and fast. His balls contracted. Stars danced before his eyes. The desire to sink his teeth into her shot through him as cum surged down his shaft. He opened his jaws wide, serum dripping from his teeth.

Somehow, he found the control to rear back, pulling out to stand on his knees behind her.

She whimpered at the loss.

"No sound," he whispered hoarsely, fisting his pulsing cock. He pumped it twice before flicking off the condom and spilling his seed all over her beautiful red ass.

They panted together as his vision returned to normal. His lust had not diminished, but the urgency to mark her had eased. He reached down and smeared his cum over her ass, parting her cheeks and working it down into her anus with his thumb.

Her throaty cry had him hard again in seconds. He wanted to take her ass, but knew better. He had no control—he'd certainly hurt her. So he settled, instead, for working her back hole, massaging the ring of muscle until it relaxed to let him in.

She gasped, tensing, but he brought his middle and index finger to her soaking pussy and slid them inside. The moment he began finger fucking both holes, she began moaning. She arched, rubbing her face on the bed, twisting her bound hands around each other.

He pumped faster, dizzy from the satisfaction of pleasuring her. When he reached his free hand beneath her hips and rubbed her clit, she went off.

Her scream pierced the air, echoing off the walls, nearly making him shift so he could join her howl.

Her internal walls squeezed his fingers, milking them over and over again. When she, at last, went limp, he eased them out and worked to untie the knot on the ropes.

"Beautiful girl," he croaked, releasing her hands and moving to her feet. He bent and kissed the back of her calf as he freed one ankle, then the other.

She didn't move.

He pulled on his jeans so his cock couldn't get any smart ideas while they slept and crawled up beside her, tugging the pillows out from under her hips. "Come here, baby." He pulled her against his chest.

She rolled into him, resting her head on his shoulder with a sweet little sigh.

He stroked her long, beautiful mane and kissed her forehead. The actions were foreign to him— he'd never cuddled a woman in his life—yet they seemed so natural and right. The awareness of the soft lushness of her naked form tucked against his crept in like prickles of fire, disturbing the tender moment. His palm sought her breast and the prickles burst into full flames.

"I need to get some clothes on you," he said gruffly, somehow managing to tear himself away from her. "Or I'll have your legs spread all night."

He picked up his t-shirt from where he'd thrown it on the floor earlier and pulled it over her head.

Her expression stalled his heart. There was an openness there, a trusting wonder in her the way her big blue eyes gazed up at him. She'd surrendered to his care. The impact of it nearly dropped him to his knees. His hands shook as he tugged the covers up and climbed in beside her.

He cupped her face and ran his thumb down her cheek, marveling at how soft her skin was, how perfect and smooth.

"It must be hard to lead a pack." Her words startled him.

He settled onto his back and pulled her up against his side, her head on his shoulder. "Yeah," he admitted. "Half the time I wonder what in the hell I'm doing. I started out as the anti-leader. I was alpha because of my size and strength, but I had no interest in leading. I didn't want to be like my father." He couldn't help the note of bitterness that came into his voice when he mentioned his dad.

"What was he like?" she asked softly.

He went rigid, his automatic instinct to shut down this line of questioning so familiar. But the conversation seemed important. The moment had weight. And he was so goddamn tired of the push-pull between him and Melissa that he didn't want to return to that.

"He's a hard-ass. Kicked me out of the pack at age sixteen for something I didn't even do."

Melissa's breath had stopped. She ran a hand lightly over his chest, her nails scraping through the hairs and sending shivers down his arms. "What did he think you did?"

"A girl got pregnant. She miscarried and her parents found out. She told them I was the father."

Melissa's hand went still. "And you weren't?"

He rubbed his face and sighed. "I wasn't. But I'd had sex with her older sister, which is probably what made her think to throw me under the bus. I admit I was a hellion. Shifter hormones are worse than a human's and mine were raging. I couldn't keep out of trouble. My father and I were always at odds, so I guess it was the final straw for him."

"What did you do?"

"I didn't have more than ten bucks in my wallet and the clothes on my back. I ran to lower elevation. I grew up in Estes Park. The entire town population is shifters—bet you didn't know that." He grinned, twisting to look at her.

Her return smile stopped his heart. "I had no idea."

"I lived as a wolf in the wild for a few weeks, hunted for food. But it's dangerous to stay in wolf form too long. You lose your mind—become savage. I eventually hitchhiked into Greeley and got a live-in job on a ranch there. Then found my way onto a construction team."

"And then you moved here?"

"Yeah. Eight years ago. There were only five shifters here then. The pack is still small."

"Have you seen your dad since?"

His throat tightened. "Yeah. He knows I'm here. I went home a couple times to see my siblings. It was tense, but we survived it. He wants me to bring my pack up to the games they host this year."

"Are you going to?"

He shrugged. "I don't want to, but I'm thinking about it. It might be nice for the pack—to meet some females for mating."

Melissa's open expression shuttered and he wished he hadn't said that. "Not for me," he amended quickly. "I have no interest in breeding at the moment." But that wasn't true. He had a ton of interest, but only in breeding the little human beside him.

He thought of his father and his pack of nearly one thousand wolves. He'd always been tense and angry. Always dealing with some crisis.

"Honestly, I hated him for a long time, but I guess I can see how embarrassing it must have been for the alpha's son to be the one running amok. No wonder he threw me out."

"But you didn't do it," Melissa burst out,

leaning up on her forearm. "Why would he believe someone else's word over his own son's? And who cares if you embarrassed him? He should care more about you than looking good in front of his pack."

Something dislodged in Cody's chest. Something that had long been frozen and immovable shifted around. He couldn't speak past the knot in his throat. Melissa's passionate defense of him felt too damn good. And quite probably undeserved.

"Did he ever believe you didn't do it?"

"Yeah. I think the girl came forward after I'd been banished. The guilt weighed on her, you know. Or maybe she stopped caring about protecting whoever had knocked her up. My younger sister tried to find me, then, but I stayed in the human world, where they had no connections. Not until word got around about a little pack in Colorado Springs did they figure out what had happened to me."

"You should forgive him."

She shouldn't have said it. It wasn't any of her business.

Cody's head jerked up in surprise.

"I won't forgive him, but you should. He sounds like an asshole, but he's still your dad."

Cody's eyes traced her face and for the first time, she saw genuine fondness there. He smiled. "I'll take that on advisement, Dr. Phil."

She laughed. "Well, if you don't, it's just hanging on you, not him. It becomes your limitation." Yeah, she was pulling a Dr. Phil, but she happened to know a lot about moving past trauma and getting on with your life.

"What do you know about it?"

She shrugged. She didn't really want to get into the whole PTSD thing now. Not when she felt so wonderful lying in Cody's arms. Her limbs were weak and rubbery from the two orgasms and she was high on all kinds of endorphins. Her ass still throbbed from the whipping—that part had been awful—but now she didn't mind the after effects. The heat and sting somehow mingled with the aftershocks of her recent climaxes to make the pain almost pleasurable.

He tugged a lock of her hair. "I have ways of making you talk."

"Oh, yeah?" Her voice sounded breathless, seductive. Not at all what she'd intended. "What torture would it be?"

"Forced orgasms. All night long. My tongue on your clit, my thumb in your ass, owning you until you begged and pleaded for me to stop."

The choked sound that came out of her mouth was a failed attempt at laughter, but her body heated, nipples stiffening, pussy growing slick and warm. Because she honestly didn't think she could take any more orgasms, she opted for the truth.

"I had a trauma last year. Some enemies of Ben kidnapped me to blackmail my sister into ruining him. Jeremy was part of it all—I owe him my life."

Cody had stiffened at the mention of Jeremy, but he didn't speak.

"I had nightmares for a while. When I saw a therapist, we worked on forgiveness. The guys who kidnapped me are dead, so there wasn't a question of justice needing to be served. The therapist thought if I could forgive everyone involved, it might free me from…" She trailed off.

Cody turned and propped himself up on an elbow. "From what?"

Her nose burned. She didn't want to cry—not tonight. Not now. "From feeling like a victim. Feeling powerless."

Cody remained very still, his brows knit. "Did it help?"

She nodded. "Yeah. I think so."

"I hope… Jesus." Cody rubbed his face. "Please tell me I didn't make you feel that way." The stricken look on his face turned her insides to a warm goo.

She touched his face. "Not once. I felt strong and sassy arguing with you. And turned on. Mostly,

I felt turned on." She dropped her eyes, suddenly shy.

Cody's grin warmed his face. He grasped her jaw in a commanding way and pulled her face toward his. "I think you know the feeling's mutual, baby," he growled before attacking her mouth.

10

Cody didn't think he'd sleep lying beside Melissa, knowing she was panty-less beneath his threadbare t-shirt, but he woke to her climbing out of the bed.

He reached for her automatically. His body didn't want to be separated from hers.

"I'll be right back." Her smile was sweet and soft. He loved this side of her, almost as he loved the feisty, back-talking girl he'd first met.

She padded to the bathroom, then returned with the rope in her hands.

"You want me to tie you up again?" he teased, interlacing his fingers behind his head as he lay on his back.

She wore a playful expression, one he hadn't seen on her before and he definitely liked it. She crawled up over him. "I'm going to tie you up."

He shook his head. "Sorry, baby. Not going to happen."

She seemed prepared for that answer, only half-listening as she unbuttoned his jeans and slid the zipper down. His cock, perpetually hard around her, sprang out.

"That's too bad," she purred, taking his cock in her delicate hand and closing her fingers around the base. "Because I was going to suck you off. But not if you're in danger of losing control…" She batted her eyelashes.

His thighs gripped from the pleasure of her touch and he groaned. Yeah, he wanted the blowjob. And yeah, he was in danger of losing control. But he doubted a little rope would hold him if it came down to it. He closed his eyes, shoving the wolf back down and drawing several cleansing breaths.

"Okay. Do it," he rasped and offered his wrists up to her. "I hope you know how to tie a good knot, baby, or you're going to get fucked into the next galaxy."

Her breath shuddered in, hands trembled as she looped the rope around his wrists. She tied a simple knot, then stopped and undid it. "Actually, I don't know my knots at all. I'd make a terrible boy scout."

She was so damn cute. He smiled and shook the loops of rope off and formed a quick pair of rope cuffs. "Hold these." When she did, he shoved his big hands through the loops. "Now pull the loose end until they're tight. That's it. Now attach the end to the headboard."

"I should've known you'd be bossy even when you're getting tied up."

He flashed a wicked grin. "Believe it, baby. I'm always in charge, whether my wrists are wrapped in rope or not."

She smiled sweetly. "We'll see."

He suspected, then, he was a goner. He was sure of it when she peeled off the nightshirt and gave him the mouthwatering view of her perky breasts with their hardened peach nipples.

"Squeeze your nipples," he rasped, cock straining, eyes glued to the hardened peaks.

She hesitated, as if debating whether she was going to take orders from him when she'd clearly been attempting to take the lead, but it seemed what he'd been suspecting about her was true—she liked to serve. Submission and surrender were natural for her, even if she thought she had to fight them.

She slid her small hands up her sides to squeeze her breasts.

"Pinch them." He sounded desperate.

She moistened her lips as she obeyed and he groaned, rolling his hips. The rope actually helped because when he yanked at his hands, the bite into his skin reminded him why he was bound.

"Lick one. Can you? Can you suck it?" Watching a woman suck anything turned him on, and there was something so dirty about her sucking herself.

Melissa cupped her breast and lifted it toward her mouth, extending her glorious pink tongue to circle her nipple, then suck it into her mouth.

"Oh, Jesus-fuck!"

She straddled his legs and lowered her mouth to his cock, her eyes glued on his face. There was something so erotic about the move—the fact that she was watching his face, his reaction so closely made it vastly more intimate. So sexy.

His hips thrust forward the moment her lips landed on the head of his cock and when she licked around the rim, he yanked the ropes so hard the bed frame groaned. He hoped the rope broke before the bed, because he'd carved it himself.

She took him deep in her throat.

Forget that—he didn't care which broke first, so long as it broke immediately. His eyes had changed color, need burned hot in his belly. The room spun and blurred, his awareness only on his straining erection and her hot, wet mouth.

The rope broke.

Dimly, he registered Melissa's shocked face, but the scent of her arousal filled his nostrils, the intoxication complete. He lunged forward and picked her up by the waist, arranging her on all fours and shoving her chest to the bed so her ass remained in the air. The rope still wound around his wrists, torn ends flapping as he gripped her hips and shoved balls deep into her delicious heat.

"Cody!" She sounded alarmed, but it only excited him. "Condom! You forgot a condom," she gasped.

He swore loudly. It came out more like a roar of anger, but he forced himself out of her, yanked the entire bedside drawer out and grabbed a foil packet. His teeth clamped down on it and he tore it open and sheathed his length.

Melissa, his beautiful mate, remained in the position he'd put her, waiting. She wanted this. That knowledge fueled his lust even hotter. His sense marginally returned, he reached around her hips and stroked her slit. "You're so fucking wet for me," he growled in approval, "You're always wet for me, aren't you?"

He slapped her clit.

"Yes," she gasped.

"Were you this wet for him?" He shouldn't have asked it, didn't mean to bring her fucking ex into the space between them, but now that he'd said it, he needed to know.

"No—never." Her husky voice answered immediately, without hesitation, and his inner wolf did the moonwalk around the bedroom.

He slapped her clit again. "Are you going to let

me fuck you?" It was a little late to ask permission but now that his mind had returned, he needed to be sure she wasn't afraid of him.

"Cody, now. I need you now."

He pushed into her and his senses exploded. Time disappeared. He fucked her hard and fast, holding her hips to brace them for his pounding thrusts. He wanted it to last forever and he needed it to end as soon as possible. The room bled to white as cum shot down his shaft. He buried himself deep and came with a shudder.

Melissa's internal muscles spasmed and squeezed around Cody in waves and lights shot in front of her eyes like a meteor shower. Cody pulled out and flipped her onto her back, as if she weighed nothing.

His inhuman appearance made her scream. His eyes were pale blue and his canine teeth had elongated into sharp points. He surged over her.

To mark her.

She started to scramble back, to run, but remembered his warning from their first night together.

Never run from an aroused wolf. Especially not an alpha.

Instead, she blocked him, planting her foot in

his belly and bracing her leg. "Cody," she begged, hoping he'd find control.

His hand found her foot and he gripped it, looking down and frowning. His eyes shot to hers and locked there. He drew two deep breaths and his irises changed back to gray, the fangs disappeared.

"I'm sorry. I'm sorry, princess." He dropped beside her on the bed, gathered her in his arms and kissed her temple and her hair.

Relief mingled with something more complex— the intensity of how much she loved being on the receiving end of Cody's affection—and her eyes filled with tears.

Cody stiffened beside her, even though there was no way he'd seen them—his face had been buried in her hair. His head jerked up and he stared at her as she blinked back the water.

"Did I hurt you?" he whispered hoarsely, brows drawn low.

She shook her head and pulled him down for a kiss.

He returned it, lips moving softly over hers, nipping her lower lip as he pulled away. "I smelled your tears." He wouldn't drop it. "I'm sorry." He rested a hand on her waist and propped himself up on one hand, gazing down at her. "I scared you, didn't I?"

"No, I'm okay. You scared me a bit. It hurt, but in a good way." Oh, hell, was she blushing? It was true, her pussy felt completely pummeled, her internal wall battered, but she loved the well-used feel. Orgasmic bliss still flowed through her limbs.

He unwound the busted ends of rope that still hung from his wrists, as if just becoming aware enough of his appendages to notice them.

"Are you hungry, baby? I know this amazing little store with the best cinnamon rolls you've ever tasted."

She beamed at him. This Cody—the gentle, considerate one, blew her mind. Was this really the same crude, dirty-talking stooge? She watched his tattooed muscles flex as he climbed off the bed and pulled on his clothes. Yes, it was the same guy. And if she was honest, she'd admit she freaking loved the dirty talk. Especially since he backed it up with the hottest action she'd ever had. Whipping included.

She hopped out of bed. "I'll just take a quick shower."

He looked over his shoulder and then stilled, eyelids dropping to half mast, expression turning hungry once more. "Don't come out without clothes on," he warned.

Her laughter turned into a shriek when he fake-lunged for her.

"I mean it. I'll keep you tied to that bed all day long, baby," he called after her.

She caught sight of herself in the bathroom mirror and stopped, seeing her reflection through new eyes. Her cheeks were flushed with excitement. Her body, while nothing she'd ever considered that special, still showed the marks of his possession—the finger marks on her hips, a few marks on her ass from the spanking the night before. The memory of that punishment sent flutters of excitement twittering in her belly. Had he really spanked her pussy?

She'd always been one to enjoy sex—her sister had called her a serial dater before Jeremy, but Cody made her feel desirable, like an absolute sex goddess.

She took a quick shower and dressed in the change of clothes she'd packed in Cody's saddlebag. Not finding a hair dryer, she didn't bother asking Cody, knowing he'd only mock her.

"Ready, beautiful girl?" Cody had cleaned the place and packed their things. He handed her the motorcycle helmet.

There went her hair. She took it without comment. Cody held his leather jacket out for her to put on. She couldn't help the way her eyebrows shot up in surprise before she accepted his help.

"Yeah, I know. I didn't think I had it in me, either."

Did he sound a little embarrassed?

She slid on the bike behind him and wrapped her arms around his waist. The ride up the mountain yesterday had been harrowing. She'd had a feeling Cody had driven the Ducati fast and loose on purpose, to shake her up. Today, he showed restraint, easing into speed, not leaning the bike as much around the bends.

They wound around unmarked mountain roads, up and down hills until they reached a little hole in the wall market, tucked into a hill in the middle of nowhere. A stump of wood carved into a bear stood near the doorway.

She pulled her helmet off and finger combed her hair. An elderly couple greeted them when they came in, and Cody headed straight to the counter to order two cinnamon rolls. He grabbed a small carton of milk from the dairy case and paid for everything at the old-fashioned register.

He led her back outside. There wasn't anywhere to sit, so he stood while she perched on the motor-cycle seat. Cody pulled one of the breakfast rolls out of the paper bag and held it up to her mouth.

It was enormous—far too big to fit in her mouth—so cream cheese frosting coated her lips when she attempted a bite.

Amusement crinkled Cody's eyes, but the way he stared at her lips sent heat curling between her legs. He didn't eat himself, seeming interested only in feeding her.

"You're right. These are the best cinnamon buns I've ever had."

"Say it again," he teased.

"Cinnamon?" She feigned innocence.

He stepped closer and stroked a hand up the back of her neck. "Say it, baby."

Somehow, the simple joke became sexual. His thumb stroked over her lower lip.

She took it in her mouth and sucked, hard.

Cody groaned, looking as if he was in pain.

"You're right," she whispered, knowing she'd turned the tables on him.

He closed his eyes, as if gathering control, then opened the carton of milk and chugged it all down.

She fished the burner phone out of her purse and checked for reception.

Cody frowned. "Who do you need to call?"

"My boss. To tell him I can't come into work tonight." When his lip curled in disbelief, she explained, "At the nightclub where I bartend."

Shock sent Cody's eyebrows flying to his hairline. "You bartend?" Disbelief rang in his tone.

She punched the keys with her thumb. "Yeah. I've been working there since I was eighteen. I thought I'd be able to quit when I became a real estate agent, but I don't make enough yet." She shrugged as Cody frowned.

Harry, her boss, didn't pick up, so she left a message about her mom being sick and hung up.

"You bartend?" He still seemed surprised.

"What? You think I don't know about hard work? I've been supporting myself since I went to college. It's good money. Pays the rent, because Lord knows, Jeremy never did."

Cody's scowl had returned in full force. "What did you see in that guy?"

She shrugged and looked away, not wanting to get into it with him.

"No, really." He grasped her jaw and turned her face to his. "Tell me what you saw in him. I need to know."

She nibbled her lower lip. "Remember I told you about being kidnapped last year?"

"Yeah."

"Well, Jeremy was one of my kidnappers. He and a friend flirted with me at the bar and I went home with them after work."

Cody looked murderous. "He *kidnapped* you? I'm going to kill him with my bare hands when we find the little bastard."

"He didn't know what he was getting into. His friend had just offered him a couple hundred dollars to get me into bed. Once they had me, it got more serious, and then he became a prisoner too. He escaped and came back for me. Freed me before they could kill me. So you see, I owe him my life."

Cody's nostrils flared and his fists clenched. "I see. So all I have to do to win you over is kidnap you and then set you free?"

She shoved at his immovable chest. "It's not funny."

"I'm not laughing, either. I am seriously going to beat that guy to a pulp."

"No, you're not. Did you not hear what I said? He saved my life."

"I think the favor—if you can call it that—has already been repaid. But for the record, I don't think you can call it saving your life when he's the one who put it in danger in the first place."

She crossed her arms over her chest. Tears were threatening, not because she was worried about Jeremy's life—which she should be—but because Cody was mocking her personal sense of honor.

"I won't kill him if it means that much to you, but I'm definitely going to beat his ass if Rabago doesn't finish him first."

A tear leaked from the outer corner of her eye. "Why is it all aggression with you wolves? You think you can resolve everything with violence. No wonder that woman we saw at the apartment building is hiding. No one is safe around you guys."

Too late, she realized the effect of her tirade on Cody. He'd gone pale, eyes wide. A muscle ticked in his jaw.

She'd touched a nerve. She hadn't meant it— not really. She didn't understand the wolf culture, and the physical aggression shocked her, but she shouldn't have judged. Comparing him to whoever abused that female was wrong. Cody wasn't frightening. He may like to impose his will through a little punishment, but it always ended with hot sex.

"Whatever happened to that female is totally out of the norm. Wolves protect their females and pups at all costs. I would die to keep you safe. I made that promise to your brother-in-law. I'm sorry if that's too aggressive for your liking, princess."

He crumpled the paper bag and milk carton into a tight ball and tossed them into a trash can, got on the bike, and started it up.

"Cody, I'm sorry. I'm just not used to your world. I shouldn't judge."

His shoulders softened and he took the helmet from her and put it on her head.

"I guess I felt judged by you. You know, about being with Jeremy."

Cody leaned his forehead against the helmet and snaked one hand around her nape. Their breath mingled. "No, I get it. You're loyal. But I can't help feeling protective. I still want to kill the fucker for you. But I won't."

11

The next morning, Melissa scrolled through the new house listings on the master real estate system. After another steamy round under the covers, Cody had left for work.

Ben had texted that he'd transferred fifteen thousand dollars to Cody's account and said they'd come straight to Colorado Springs on Friday, hopefully arriving before the meet-up with Rabago, which Rabago had set for Friday evening in an abandoned lot on the edge of town. She needed to make sure Jeremy was at that meeting too, or else Rabago would probably keep looking for him. She had an idea about where he might be. He had a cousin who lived in Denver. He might have gone there to lie low. She texted him about the money and the meeting, but still hadn't heard from him.

To distract herself while she waited for a reply, she skimmed through the new listings now.

Her focus shot to a new listing in the Old North End neighborhood. A CJ Steele house! Excitement sped through her veins as she scanned the details. The house was only two blocks from Cody's place, which meant she could probably slip out and take a peek without him ever knowing she'd been gone. Rabago wouldn't find her, not on such a short jaunt. Even if Cody found out, it would be worth it. Hell, she'd welcome that kind of interaction with him after the distant cold treatment she'd received the day before.

She picked up the burner cell phone and dialed the dickwad listing realtor Brad Johnson to express her interest. He somehow managed to sound both bored and condescending, giving her the key code, but acting as if he knew the house was out of her price range. Which it was—at least the range she felt comfortable borrowing from her brother-in-law.

Dressed in a skirt and blouse in case she ran into other realtors while she was there, she slipped on her heels and went out Cody's back door, just in case someone was watching the house. Which was highly unlikely. If Rabago knew where she was, he'd have broken the door down already.

She walked purposefully down the sidewalk, taking long strides and enjoying the warm summer sun. She spotted the house immediately. Like all CJ

Steele homes, the yard was impeccably manicured with native trees, shrubs, and flowers, the house gleamed with cobalt blue paint, setting off the old brick. Using the keypad on the electronic Supra lockbox, she opened it and retrieved the key. She pushed the door open, stepped inside and smiled.

Beautiful.

Hard wood floors. Exposed brick walls. Every detail was perfect, as she knew it would be. She rounded the bend into the kitchen and stopped short with a gasp.

Cody turned from the window with a paintbrush in his hand, obviously touching up a last little bit of paint. He straightened when he saw her.

"What are you doing here?" she spluttered. Of course, he ought to be the one asking that question, but she had to say something.

He walked around to the sink and rinsed off his brush. "I could ask you the same, princess."

"I know, I'm sorry. But it's a CJ Steele house, and it just came on the market today. I've been dreaming of owning one for years, and this is my chance. I didn't want to miss out."

Cody hadn't looked up from the sink, so she continued with her explanation. "Plus, it was so close. I mean, you only live a couple blocks away. I was careful. I mean, there was no one out to see me or anything."

He finished with the brush and wiped out the

sink with a rag, polishing the brushed aluminum faucet and handles before he dropped the brush and the rag onto a work tray.

"You're in trouble, baby. That's all I have to say."

Her belly fluttered. Despite her protests, she actually loved their dance of dominance and submission. "Am I?"

He crossed to a window to close the blinds. "I think punishment at the scene of the crime is most fitting." He removed the plastic tilt wand and slapped it in his palm like an old-fashioned teacher swishing a cane. He lifted his chin toward the polished concrete countertop. "Hands on the counter. Ass out."

Her pussy clenched. "Cody, someone could walk in."

"I won't let anyone see you, I promise. I have shifter hearing. I would notice anyone coming long before they got to the door. But just think--there could've been far worse consequences to you leaving the house. Someone could've seen you. Someone could have picked you up and tortured you, mutilated your body, and dumped it as a message for your ex."

She shuddered and glared at him for making his description so extreme.

"This consequence will be mild, in comparison." The familiar glint of hunger showed on his face and she flushed with heat. If Cody enjoyed it, she knew she would too. After he made her suffer a little.

And suffering for Cody's pleasure somehow didn't bother her nearly as much as she thought it should. In fact, the idea had her nipples hard beneath her blouse, panties growing damp.

Cody's big hand clapped down on her ass and stayed there. He squeezed.

Her breath left her throat in a rush.

Both his palms spanned her bare thighs and slid upward, dragging her skirt with them.

Her pussy clenched, heat flooding her pelvis and running down her legs.

When he had her skirt hiked up over her waist, he hooked his thumbs in the waistband of her panties and dragged them down to her ankles.

"You're going to hold still for me this time, baby." Even though the words sounded rough, his voice caressed her body, the heat in them smoldering, leaving her scorched and raw.

She wanted him. She wanted this, as crazy as that was. She needed it, craved it.

She leaned on her forearms and pushed her ass out for him.

The wand made a hiss as it sliced through the air. When it struck her bare flesh, she screamed. The thin line of impact burned like fire.

Cody swung it again and it struck just below the first line. She let out a whimper.

"You've been *bad*, baby." Cody's deepened voice seemed to reach right into her. The words dripped with suggestion. "Arch your back, show me that ass."

Whap. Another line of fire. She danced on her feet.

"Spread your legs apart. Farther." His voice came low and close this time.

She widened her stance.

He applied the crop-like implement one more time.

When she opened her eyes—she didn't remember closing them—her breath was still coming in ragged pants.

She felt the touch of something cold and hard between her legs and started. Cody had threaded the wand through them and he rubbed her wet pussy with it. "You love my punishments." There was an accusation in his voice and she knew they were talking about yesterday's conversation.

"Yes." No point in lying. She needed something from him now—desperately.

He wrapped his fingers in her hair and tugged her head back. The wand continued to stroke slowly over her clit. "You don't like obeying, though."

THE SCENT of Melissa's arousal filled the room, sending tingles all over Cody's flesh, making his cock thicken in his jeans.

"If you were my mate, I'd follow that spanking up with a long, hard punishment fuck."

Her eyes dilated. She moistened her lips and the sight of her tongue nearly drove him wild. "What's that?"

He leaned down and nipped her earlobe. "That's where I fuck you until you scream your release and then I turn you over and fuck your ass until you forget your name."

She wobbled on her feet. "Cody," she whispered hoarsely, "my legs won't hold me up."

He couldn't help it—he was back in explicit crude mode. "Maybe because you belong on your knees."

He expected to see irritation or disgust on her face, but she held his eyes and lowered to her knees. He sucked in a shocked breath. Her fingers unfastened the button of his jeans and urged the zipper down until his cock sprang free.

She wasted no time fisting the base of his cock and taking it into her mouth.

He shuddered with pleasure.

She sucked hard and bobbed her head on and

off fast. Then she slowly, deliberately, took him all the way to the back of her throat and out again.

His thighs shook. "That's it, baby. Show me how sorry you are."

She came off and licked a long line from his balls to the head of his cock, then around the rim.

He twined his fingers in her hair and pushed her forward.

Her eyes widened in surprise, so he stopped short of hitting the back of her throat. Gripping her head with both his hands, he held it still and pumped his length into her mouth, using her like a fuck hole.

She liked that. He caught another waft of her beautiful musk.

He closed his eyes, his control slipping. Her fingernails dug into his thighs.

"I'm going to come," he warned before he came like a space shuttle hurtling to the moon.

She kept her lips closed around his cock, took his seed and swallowed it down.

Damn.

"Melissa, that was incredible."

She came off and bit his thigh.

His vision domed immediately, teeth dropped. Female wolves bit and scratched during sex and it fully activated the beast within him.

To keep from marking her, he whirled and

walked several steps away, shoving his cock back in his jeans and zipping them.

When he turned, Melissa looked lost on her knees alone and he felt like an asshole. He strode over, picked her up by the armpits and tossed her over his shoulder, yanking her skirt back down and picking up her panties from the floor.

"It's time for your ass-fucking."

"Cody." She sounded slightly alarmed. "Please."

He shoved her panties in his pocket, picked up the work tray and marched out the front door, locking it behind him.

"Cody, put me down! This is unseemly. Please don't carry me like this."

Hearing her desperation, he dropped her to her feet, then swung her back up in a cradle position. Her eyes widened in surprise.

"Better?"

She hesitated, then nestled her head onto his shoulder, against his neck in a move that turned his insides to liquid. "Yes."

He made it to his house in less than a minute and unlocked the door, still refusing to put her down. He carried her into the bedroom, where he dropped her on her feet, spun her around, and unzipped her fitted yellow skirt. It dropped to the floor in a pastel puddle.

"Cody, I don't think this is a good idea. I mean, do you think it's safe?"

He decided not to take her blouse and bra off, to assist in keeping control. Placing his hand on her back, he bent her torso down over the bed.

"Cody, wait!"

He squeezed her welted cheeks. "Bad girls get fucked in the ass, baby."

"Cody!"

The panic in her voice made him lean over and whisper, "What's wrong, baby? Do you think I don't know how to make it good for you?"

The tension in her body eased.

"Hmm?"

"No," she agreed.

"Have I ever left you unsatisfied?"

"No."

After retrieving a bottle of lubricant from his bathroom medicine chest, he massaged a generous dollop into her anus, stretching it with his forefinger. He inserted a second finger and moved them in and out. With his other hand, he rubbed a circle around her clit.

"What happens to bad girls, princess?"

She answered with a moan.

He withdrew the fingers from her ass, but kept teasing her clit, using her ample natural lubrication to slick the way. With his right hand, he slapped her ass. "I asked you a question."

"They get spanked!" she cried.

He chuckled. "Yes, they do. Every time. And where do they get fucked?"

She moaned again.

He spanked again.

"In the ass! They get fucked in the ass."

"That's right, baby. Do you want me to fuck you in the ass?"

She whimpered. "No."

He stilled the fingers on her clit.

"Yes. Yes, I do."

"I thought so." He pushed the head of his cock against her anus.

"No-o," she moaned, squeezing her anus against the intrusion.

"Take it, baby," he ordered, although he didn't apply any pressure.

She immediately softened, relaxing the tight ring of muscle and allowing his cock to enter. She moaned as the thickest part of his head pushed past her anus, and then he was in.

He rocked slowly in and out of her.

"Ung… uh… oh…" Her little sounds drove him mad.

"Take it," he repeated, picking up his speed. He wrapped his left hand around her waist and tapped her clit.

"Oh!" The tinge of orgasm sounded in her cry.

He worked her clit, then reached further and plunged the cone of his fingers into her pussy.

She shrieked with alarmed enthusiasm.

"Who owns you right now?"

"You do," she gasped. "Oh, please, it's too much!"

He closed his eyes and let the pleasure overcome him. Her scent, the tight fit in her ass, the wetness of her pussy around his fingers. Shoving deep, he came with a shout.

Melissa's hands shot down between her legs and she thrust his fingers in deeper, her internal walls contracting around them.

The evidence of her orgasm sent another release blasting through him. When he'd spent, he folded over her, nibbling on her ear. The gentle waves of bliss resulting from his release cleared away all the walls he'd put up over the past twenty-four hours to keep her out. Was he seriously willing to give up this? He'd never felt so connected, so right. Even the discomfort of holding back from marking her was worth the pleasure of moving inside her, of holding her in his arms afterward.

He eased out of her and scooped her into his arms, carrying her into the shower where he turned the spray on both of them.

Melissa wobbled on her feet, so he held her up with an arm around her waist, spooning her from behind as she stood facing the spray of water. After a moment, he gently rotated her to rinse her back, running his hands down her back, parting her cheeks to wash away his seed.

Her arms looped around his neck and she clung there, as if he was the buoy that kept her from washing out to sea. He kissed her temple, her jaw, her hair. He found himself wanting to whisper promises to her, but nothing came to mind that he could keep.

She didn't belong to him—wasn't his mate. He'd already determined it wouldn't work between them. Why then, did his body seem so desperate to keep her?

AN HOUR LATER, Cody was manning the grill. It seemed to be the only kind of cooking he did, which was fine with her. He looked damn good when he did it, his t-shirt fitting tight over the muscles of his chest, ass sexy in those faded blue jeans.

He noticed her watching from the porch and smiled. The boyish grin lacked all of the cocky attitude he'd given her when they first met, the openness in his face a startling difference.

How had she changed?

She'd just lost her anal virginity—that was huge. But more than that, it seemed like he'd knocked down the walls she had, refinished her like one of his CJ Steele homes. Structurally, she remained the same, but everything inside had changed.

Cody piled a stack of bratwurst onto a plate and met her on the steps. His hand fell on her ass and he squeezed.

She sucked in her breath over her teeth.

He didn't let go, stroking and squeezing again. "Sore, baby?"

She tried to muster some indignation at his rubbing it in, but instead only that gooey melting of her will happened. Surrender.

Still holding the plate of food with one hand, he burrowed his fingers into her hair, tipped her face up to his and claimed her mouth with a hard, punishing kiss. "Come on," he murmured. "I'll feed you."

He'll feed her.

Since when did men feed her? When had anyone looked after her half as well as he had? Yeah, there had been the Walmart clothing fiasco, but in retrospect, she saw the humor in it. His protection and care had come grudgingly first, but now she was sure he enjoyed her company. Or maybe it was just post-coital bliss talking.

She followed him inside and watched him fork three sausages onto buns on a plate and hand it to her.

"Whoa, that's too many," she protested.

He smirked and took two back. "Just a one-sausage girl, princess?"

She slapped his chest. "Would you stop with your cocky—"

He cut off her tirade with another kiss.

She melted after a moment, moving her lips against his, allowing his tongue entry. "I'll stop," he said softly when he pulled away. "Why don't you take these to the couch?" He handed her two plates of food. "Want a glass of wine?"

She stopped on her way to the couch. "Do you have any?" All she'd seen was Budweiser in the fridge.

He grinned. "I might have a bottle stashed around here for when I want to woo a woman."

She tossed her still-damp hair over her shoulder. "Is that what you're doing now?"

"Maybe."

Then why don't you mark me?

Dang, did she really want him to mark her? To spend the rest of her life as his mate? That couldn't be. She just didn't like the sense of inadequacy produced by his determination not to mark her.

Cody walked over and handed her a glass of pinot noir and a bag of potato chips with salt and vinegar, just the way she liked them.

She snapped it open and dumped a handful on each of their plates while he returned to the kitchen for his beer.

"So did you like the house? What you saw of it?" He smirked, probably remembering how her visit to the house had ended.

"Yes. I'm going to put an offer on it."

"Are you? How much?"

"Well, it's a little out of my range, but I'm going to go full price and submit the offer tonight, otherwise I'll lose it."

He gave her a curious look and rubbed a smudge of mustard from his lower lip. "Nah. You should lowball it. Offer the price you can afford. You never know, he might take it."

She shook her head. "I don't want to lose this house. They don't come around that often, and I need a place to live right away. The timing is perfect. Besides, his agent is an ass, remember? He would laugh in my face if I submitted a lowball offer."

Cody stared at her with an odd expression for a moment, then applied himself to eating his brat. "Are you sure it's the right house?" he asked after a moment. "It's pretty small."

She snorted. "Like I could afford any bigger. No, it's perfect. Just what I've always dreamed of."

Cody looked thoughtful as he inhaled his food but he didn't mention it again. After they ate, she washed the plates and set them in the drying rack, poured a fresh glass of wine, and sat on the couch with her Chromebook to send Brad Johnson the offer on the house while she watched a movie.

Cody plunked down beside her, tossed an arm around her shoulders. What are you looking to watch? Want me to drive?"

She rolled her eyes, but handed over the remote. She didn't watch much television and sucked at figuring out what to watch. "Chick flick," she said, just to test his reaction.

Both his eyebrows raised. "Are you serious?"

"Not really. I don't care." She cracked open the Chromebook to prepare the paperwork.

"You don't care? Come on, give me more to work with than that."

"I honestly don't care."

He frowned at her. "Chick flick it is," he groaned.

12

Cody picked up Stone's money from his bank. He'd felt like a bank robber, packing all that cash into a duffel bag that he stowed under the seat of his truck.

Afterward, he drove to Starbucks. He could hardly believe he was doing it, but Melissa had asked about coffee the first morning and he'd blown off her request every day since. She deserved it after putting up with his overbearing crap.

After the way she'd surrendered.

He'd been up the night before, staring at the text from his realtor, Brad Johnson, about her offer on the house. On one hand, he wanted her to have it. He'd loved her perspective about there being a perfect buyer for a house. Someone who would love it as much as he did. Yes, he wanted Melissa living in one of his houses.

The trouble was, he wasn't sure he wanted her in *that* house.

He'd been starting to picture her in a different house altogether. One he'd love remodeling just for her. And him.

The thought of keeping Melissa, marking her and making her his made his shifter blood sing. The wolf wanted her. The wolf didn't seem to care that she was only one quarter shifter. That their children would probably never be able to shift. That he'd lose his position as alpha because his mate was weak.

But beyond his intense physical need for her, there was more. He'd begun to understand her better. His initial assessment of her as a diva may have been off. She worked weekends as a bartender to get by—she was no stranger to hard work. She'd put up with a loser boyfriend out of a fierce sense of loyalty. He may think it was totally misplaced, but he admired the hell out of the sentiment. She bonded like a shifter.

She was sweet as honey when he wasn't being an asshat and despite her frequent displays of defiance, had an innate response to dominance. Every time he'd won her surrender had been spectacular. Tender. Beautiful. He'd never felt so connected to another being—shifter or human—in his life.

So yeah, she deserved coffee this morning. And

if he could wrap his mind around how to make it work mating her, a house.

He got out of his car to stand in line, staring at the board with the huge array of choices. Damn. He should've asked what kind of coffee drink she liked instead of trying to surprise her with it when she woke.

For the first time, ever, he really cared about making a female—his female—happy.

His phone rang and he frowned, glancing at a number he didn't recognize.

"This is Steele."

"I need your help." He recognized the tight, desperate voice immediately. The new female shifter in town.

"What is it?" he asked sharply.

"Jayden—my son—he was hit by a car. The humans took him to a hospital in an ambulance."

"And now you'll be found by whomever you're running from," he finished. Unless the car had crushed his skull, the boy would recover from the car accident in no time. Far too quickly for doctors to understand. What's more, his mother would have to show identification and give his name or risk alerting Child Protective Services.

"Yes."

"Where are you now?"

"St. Francis."

"I'll be right there."

He abandoned the coffee shop and climbed in his truck. For a brief moment, he considered picking up Melissa, because she might be better at soothing the distraught mother, but then realized how dangerous it would be for her to get in the middle of a shifter war.

He texted her as he drove off, letting her know the situation and telling her to sit tight and contact him if she had an emergency.

As he drove to the hospital, he remembered the boy. Jayden had had the look of a beaten street dog. Signs of past abuse were in his wary eyes and gaunt face, but the way he watched Cody, responded to his offer of money showed he was smart and eager to please. He needed to help these three. He'd be damned if he let whoever had them scared pick them up out of his territory.

He dialed the number Colleen—or whatever her real name was—had called him from when he arrived at St. Francis and found the terrified family in a small exam room in the children's ward. No doctors or nurses were around to see them, so he wasted no time and asked no questions. He simply scooped the boy up, craned his neck to make sure the corridor was clear, and carried the boy out. The boy's mom and sister followed tight on his heels, on board with his silent departure.

"What happened, kid?" he asked as he jogged

down the stairs, having decided the elevator was too public for their escape.

He scented fear on the boy, who must be around ten or eleven years old. "I got hit by a car," he mumbled.

"What hurts?"

"My head. And my leg was broken." He used the past tense because the leg would already be mostly healed, although the family seemed malnourished, which would affect his ability to regenerate. It explained why his mother's missing teeth had only partially regrown.

"You'll feel better in a few hours." He opened the passenger side door to his pickup truck and tilted the seat forward to let the mother and girl climb in the back. "What's your name?"

"Jayden."

"How about you?" he asked the girl.

"Angie."

He dropped the boy on the front seat and shut the door. It didn't appear anyone had noticed their hasty departure.

"How far would they be coming from?" he asked Colleen as he pulled out of the hospital parking lot.

"Kentucky." Her voice cracked.

"How many?"

"The pack is huge—a hundred fifty members. If only the men came, it would be eighty or ninety."

He gritted his teeth. His pack would be no match for them. Ben's could handle them, however. The question was, did he want this to be his return favor from the guy? He didn't relish releasing that debt quite so soon and for something that wasn't really his deal. But he wasn't going to leave this woman unprotected, either.

"I'm going to take you back to my place until we figure out the best strategy. I might want to hide you up in Denver where there's a bigger pack to protect you if there's trouble."

She shook her head. "Bigger pack means more wolves who might know… him. Or talk."

"We'll take that into consideration." Irritation with the situation in general made his tone sharper than he meant.

In the rearview mirror, he saw her flinch and duck her head. "Sorry, Alpha."

He blew out his breath in exasperation. He was trying to win her trust, not bully her into submission. "Forgiven," he muttered.

He pulled up at his place and carried the boy inside, Colleen and Angie trailing behind.

Melissa met them at the door, brow furrowed with concern. She bustled around, offering food and beverage, and when they were refused, preparing a plate of pancakes, sliced apples, and a pile of strawberries, anyway. She dropped them on the coffee table with syrup, plates, and forks.

The kids immediately reached for the food, devouring everything in five minutes flat. Melissa picked it up and prepared a second plate, which she brought with glasses of orange juice.

He said little, working on finding a show on the television to occupy the kids so the adults could talk, watching Melissa with gratitude. Her cheery small talk filled the space, easing the tension and distracting the children.

MELISSA NOTICED Cody wore that vaguely concerned look he'd worn during the pack meeting, like too much rode on his shoulders and he wanted to get it all right.

"Let's talk out on the back porch—the kids are fine in here," he said.

She stood up, then hesitated, not sure if he meant her, too, or if he wanted privacy talking to Colleen.

He caught her indecision and nodded. "You can come, too." To Colleen, he said, "She's a friend of the pack and under our protection. She can be trusted."

Colleen didn't quite meet her eye, but mumbled, "She's part wolf."

"How did you know?" she asked in surprise.

The female shrugged. "I can just tell."

Cody gave a vague smile. "Your wolf instincts are better than mine; I didn't guess it right away."

"I've had to use them for survival on a daily basis."

They sat down on the back steps, since Cody didn't own any patio furniture.

He rested his forearms on his knees, hands caged loosely between them. "So what's your story?"

The woman didn't seem taken aback by his bluntness. Maybe it was a shifter thing. Her brother-in-law was pretty direct, too. She remembered Ashley calling her the day she met him and likening him to Batman with his brooding, monosyllabic authority.

Colleen smoothed her blonde hair, fidgeting with the ends. She had blue-green eyes and a pretty, heart-shaped face. Melissa had originally pegged her as older because of the strain around her mouth and eyes, but now that she observed, the woman seemed too young to have children half-grown. She couldn't be much older than Melissa.

"Our alpha wants us back. He's my mate. Or at least, he thinks he is." Something in the stony way she said the last sentence gave a glimpse of the steel that lay beneath that kicked dog vibe.

Melissa almost smiled.

"You left him." Cody's words sounded more like a statement than question.

Colleen nodded. "My sister helped us get away after he beat Jayden so badly he didn't heal for school."

She felt the blood drain from her face.

Cody's eyes flicked to hers, and she remembered their quarrel from the day before. She'd been wrong. Cody was nothing like this woman's husband, or mate—whatever she called him. Only a monster would beat a child like that.

"We've been on the run for a month. I haven't been able to get much work, other than cleaning houses. I didn't want to use my I.D. anywhere, in case he could trace it." She shrugged her slender shoulders. "I don't know how these things work."

"I'm not sure, either. I think if he's filed a missing person report on the three of you, then there is a chance you showing up at that hospital will alert the police in his area. We have a friend in law enforcement who might be able to fill us in."

"I appreciate your help. Both of you." She looked at Melissa. "You were really nice to my pups, and it's been a long time since we've seen a friendly face." Her eyes swam with tears.

Melissa moved to sit closer to her, hesitating, then putting a tentative hand on her back and rubbing. "We won't let anyone take you or your kids," she promised, meeting Cody's eye to demand his agreement.

"No, we won't." His sober gaze rested on her

face and she saw such honor and kindness there it nearly undid her.

AFTER EVERYONE ATE the pizza Cody had ordered for dinner, he dragged Melissa into the garage for a word in private. Her comment the day before about violence had put him on the defensive, but now, being up close and personal with domestic abuse, he needed to try to explain things to her.

She looked at him expectantly, her big eyes watchful.

"Listen, Melissa." He stabbed his fingers through his hair. "What you said yesterday—"

"I'm sorry," she cut in. "I know it's not the same."

A rush of warmth went through him. She'd been amazing with the family—working to put Colleen at ease and make the children comfortable. She may not be a shifter, but she had the sort of hostess/pack mother skills that made her the perfect mate for an alpha.

"We are… physical. That's true. We heal quickly, so showing physical dominance never causes anyone lasting harm."

A shadow crossed her face.

"A dominant male is the most aggressive, but he also has a built-in need to protect—especially those much weaker than him, like pups." He gestured toward the house. It made him sick to think of an alpha wolf abusing those poor children. "And the mechanism to ensure a female's safety is simple. Her tears trigger an instant response in her mate. They calm all aggression and produce a powerful need to solve whatever problem is making her cry. In a situation like Colleen's, something's gone terribly wrong. A wolf would have to be sick in the head to hurt his own pups and mate like that."

"That makes sense. Like I said, I shouldn't have judged. It's just new to me."

"I hope I haven't scared you or made you feel unsafe. That was never my intention."

She shook her head. "You haven't. You're just...cocky and overbearing. Honestly, I think I'm more disturbed by how much it turns me on than by anything you've done."

His lips curved as he stepped closer to her. "Baby, I don't know what this thing is between us, but—"

"It's just sex," she said too quickly.

He winced. "I don't think so," he said in a low voice. "My inner wolf has been screaming for me to mark you since the first time we touched."

She let out a soft chuff. "Mate me? A human? Wouldn't that screw up your ability to lead the pack?" He heard the bitterness in her voice, and was surprised she knew enough about pack dynamics to understand.

"Yeah. I know. I've been fighting it, but—"

Her brows knit and he realized too late that he'd said the wrong thing. She stiffened and worked to swallow. "It's just sex," she said firmly.

"Hang on." He reached for her but she slipped out of his grasp.

"No, you're right. You should definitely fight it. A mating bite could be dangerous to a human. I can't risk my life to be permanently mated to some construction worker I just met. That would be nuts."

Her words hit him like a cement block to the chest. He may have been thinking the same thing about it just being sex, but now… he felt so much more for her. To hear that she still thought he was so far beneath her was a huge blow to his ego. No, it was more than that, but he couldn't even consider the implications of a true mate who didn't return his affections at the moment.

"Right, princess. Well, don't worry. Tomorrow you can stop slumming it with me and go back to your picture-perfect life." He stalked past her and into the house.

MELISSA'S EYES BURNED. She hadn't meant to wound Cody—not at all. She'd been protecting herself, defending against her growing desire to be… loved by Cody. Claimed by Cody. She wanted him to mark her, more and more every time they were together, every interaction they had, every moment she witnessed his gentle leadership and power.

If she was totally honest with herself, she'd recognize that she'd already fallen in love with him, somewhere between the way he held her that first night when she'd been crying and watching movies together the night before.

But he looked down on humans. He didn't want to be mated to her, despite their mutual attraction. She wasn't going to cut his legs off him when he was so new at leading a pack and letting go of his father's worst opinion of him.

So she'd given him an out.

She never expected to see him so affected by her words. He'd paled, fists balled at his sides, muscle ticking in his jaw.

Blinking back tears, she entered the house softly. It had gone quiet—the living room was empty, save for the giant silver wolf curled up by the door, looking pointedly away from her.

Cody must have given his bedroom to Colleen and her children, which left the couch for her.

"Cody?"

The wolf ignored her.

"I didn't mean—"

Cody's lips curled back and he bared his fangs, issuing a low growl. She froze, every human instinct screaming *run for your life*, even though she knew he wouldn't harm her. She did lose what remained of her courage to try to talk to him, though.

She sat on the couch and hugged a pillow, knowing she probably wouldn't get a wink of sleep.

13

She woke with a stiff neck and a pain in her heart. The Kentucky family were whispering in the bedroom, obviously staying in until they were sure she was up. No sign of Cody.

She made a lot of noise as she headed to the shower, to let Cody's other guests know it was safe to come out. When she emerged, Colleen stood in the kitchen, her hand on the refrigerator door, looking unsure.

"I don't know where Cody went, but he would want you to help yourself to anything," she said.

"Oh, okay." She appeared relieved. "I'm going to make some eggs, would you like some?"

"That sounds great, thanks." She let Colleen do her thing in the kitchen.

Hoping to cheer herself with good news, she

checked her email, but CJ Steele's agent hadn't replied to her offer. Which meant it had expired.

That was bullshit—it was a full-priced offer and the house was still listed on the market. She grabbed her phone and dialed Brad Johnson, the agent.

"Yes, this is Melissa Bell, I put in the offer on the CJ Steele Old North End house two days ago?"

The agent grunted.

"Why wasn't it accepted? Do you have another offer?"

"No, I don't have another offer. I'm sorry yours expired before the owner had a chance to make up his mind. You should have given the offer more time for consideration."

She blew out her breath. "What was there to consider if it was full price and there wasn't another offer?"

Brad made a sound of impatience. "To be perfectly frank, I got the feeling it had something to do with you, personally."

A wash of cold went over her. Had he black-balled her permanently because of that first stupid deal? It wouldn't be fair. All she ever wanted was a positive relationship with the man. And to live in one of his houses.

"Excuse me?"

"I don't know. He said he had to think about it

—he wasn't sure if this house was right for you, or something."

The cold turned into a prickly heat. "Is there any way I can contact him? Speak to him directly?"

"You know I'm not going to give out his personal information." The condescension in his voice made her want to kick him in the shins.

She hung up without saying goodbye and hit the mousepad on her Chromebook. There had to be some listing of the guy's phone number somewhere. On county tax records, or on the business license or something. She Googled CJ Steele Construction, and that easily produced a number.

Her thumb flew over the keypad dialing it and she stood up and paced past the picture windows, knowing the children were probably listening to every word.

The screen flashed the name 'Cody' as the ringtone sounded both from the phone and, muffled, from the garage.

Cody's voice came on. "I'm in the garage."

Her heart surged to her throat.

She punched the end button and stared at the blank screen in the biggest WTF moment of her life.

Cody was CJ Steele?

No… maybe that was just the number Steele had used to list his company. But even before she finished the thought, she discarded it. Cody had to be Steele. It was so obvious now, it killed her. *C* stood for Cody.

Why in the hell hadn't he told her? Anger boiled, hot and thick.

She marched to the garage and threw open the door.

Cody had his Ducati up on stands, doing some kind of maintenance or repair.

She shut the door behind her, not wanting to give Colleen and her kids a show. "So, I bet you thought it was hilarious to string me along. *Make a lowball offer on the house*, you advised."

Cody stood and wiped the grease from his hands with a rag. His expression turned shuttered.

"You couldn't wait to put me in my place, could you?"

"Now hold on—" he started.

"You've been dying to since the moment we first met." She spread her arms wide. "You think I'm a spoiled little princess who can't break a fingernail. I guess you've had a load of laughs while I've waxed on about the great and famous CJ Steele."

His eyes narrowed. "I don't really see why you're mad here. Shouldn't it be me?"

Her mouth opened and closed. "Why would you be mad? You could buy and sell half this city. All I wanted was one damn house, and I was willing to pay full price for it."

Cody's brow furrowed.

"But you couldn't wait to drop this on my head. Does it feel good? Now you can lord the thing I want most over me? Make me grovel for it. Is that what you want?" She put her hands on her hips. "Because I will. I know that's what you like, isn't it?"

His face flushed and eyes flashed to light blue, anger lighting his face. "I don't see where you get off. You're the one who thinks she's too good for me, the lowly *construction worker*. You won't even consider me as a mate. Am I worthy now? Is it different when you know I have money?"

Hot with shame and humiliation rushed over her. He was right. She had misjudged him. Maybe that was part of why she was so mad—her own prejudice embarrassed her.

"No," she snapped. "Money can't fix a jerk." Spinning on her heel, she flew back into the house and slammed the door behind her.

In the garage, the sound of a metal tool clattering against a wall and then the concrete floor echoed.

Her phone dinged at the same time a knock sounded on the front door. She looked down at the screen.

Ashley had texted, "We're here!"

Not one minute too soon. She jogged to the door and threw it open. Ignoring the two huge men —shifters—beside her sister, she snatched her up in a hard hug.

~

Cody cursed and picked up another wrench to throw, but the scent of two male wolves made him stiffen and he charged inside, instead.

Melissa stood clasped in an embrace with a woman who looked identical to her, except with hair a few inches shorter. Beside them stood Mark Ruhl, whose scent he would have recognized had his brain been clearer, and the wolf who must be Ben Stone.

"We came back early," Ben said, by way of greeting. "I wanted to get Melissa out of Colorado Springs before the payoff." He and Mark remained outside on the step, showing deference to Cody's territory as alpha of his town.

"Come in."

Ben entered and held out his palm, which Cody shook first, before Mark's. "Thank you for your help. I'm in your debt."

He tried to stay focused on Ben, but his gaze kept sliding to Melissa, his gut twisting. She'd be leaving now.

He never had to see her again.

Every cell in his body rebelled at the idea. His wolf itched to snatch her up and hold her tight against him, to refuse to let her leave his premises. Ever.

But it couldn't be. They'd just proven over and

over again they were utterly incompatible. She didn't care about him—thought he was beneath her. And he shouldn't care about her. Shouldn't want a human.

He caught Stone's sharp gaze and gave himself a mental shake. Melissa had moved inside, and seemed to be making quick work of packing her things.

"How does that sound to you?"

"I'm sorry—what?"

Don't let her leave, his wolf growled.

Both his new guests had also lost focus on the conversation as they caught Colleen's scent. Mark gaped at her where she had shrunk back in the kitchen as if to hide.

With effort, Cody tore his attention away from Melissa and beckoned Colleen forward. "Colleen, come here, please."

Her green eyes appeared wary, but she obeyed, walking slowly into the room as she wiped her hands on her jeans. Her children, who had been playing on his computer in the bedroom, also emerged, standing in the doorway of the bedroom.

Mark's expression had turned predatory, and Colleen responded to his interest, tugging her blond hair out of its ponytail and letting it fall across her shoulders.

"This is Colleen. She and her children may need more protection than my pack can provide."

"They can stay with me." Mark spoke before he'd even finished his last word, before even hearing what she needed protection from.

It was fine with him. He couldn't focus, couldn't think as his wolf clawed and scrabbled just beneath the surface.

Don't. Let. Her. Leave.

He was sweating, the pain of transition as sharp as if the moon were still full.

Melissa hadn't looked at him as she moved about the place, gathering up her things. She'd packed a duffel bag. Where it came from, he wasn't sure.

"If you want out of it, my pack can handle the meet," Stone was saying. His words sounded dim over the blaring in his ears.

He shook his head. "I'll handle the meet."

"You sure?"

"I'm sure."

"Ruhl will go with you, with backup from my pack. Yours, too, if you like. I'll take the females and pups back to Denver until it's over."

Not my female.

But she wasn't his female. He hadn't marked her. Dammit! Why hadn't he marked her? At that moment, he didn't care that she was human, or whether she thought he was good enough for her. He'd give her everything she ever wanted. The house of her dreams. Clothes, makeup. Flowers.

He'd treat her like the fucking princess she was. Why had he mocked her with the name that suited her so well?

The room spun around him, too warm.

No, Melissa had to go. She needed to get out of harm's way, Stone was right. He would protect her like his own mate. She was his family.

He drew several deep breaths to clear his vision. Stone watched him with an assessing look. Ruhl was deep in conversation with Colleen, who looked five years younger now as she smiled shyly up at him.

Melissa walked past him and put her hand on the doorknob. "I'll pay you back for the stuff you bought me as soon as I get paid."

"I don't want your money. Melissa—"

She stopped, her blue-eyed stare slamming into him with the force of a wrecking ball.

His mind went blank. The animal tore too close to the surface for coherent thoughts to be expressed.

Her lips turned down. "See you around." The soft murmur oozed sadness, defeat.

He'd done that to her. Ripped her down, acted like a defensive teenager. Was he still that proud, stupid kid his father had thrown out on his ass twelve years ago? Did he need to prove something to the world? To Melissa? Or was it to his father? Was he still trying to earn his approval by mating an alpha female instead of the woman he loved? Yes—
loved.

Fuck that.

He was alpha. He didn't need to prove anything to anyone. If he wanted a beautiful redhead quarter-breed, he should claim her.

But she was walking down the sidewalk, away from him. And she hadn't looked back. Not once.

His chest seared like it had been ripped open, but he froze, letting her walk away. Out of his house and out of his life.

This was wrong. So wrong.

MELISSA ONLY HELD it together because Colleen and her kids were with them. She pasted a tight smile on her face and climbed in the back seat of Ben's shiny black SUV. Even so, both Ashley and Colleen sent her sympathetic glances.

She hadn't fooled anyone.

"Don't give up on him," Colleen murmured.

Her eyebrows shot to her hairline.

The woman blushed. "I know—I don't know either of you, but I couldn't help overhear your fight. And I know he cares about you."

She swallowed. *Cared* about? Or liked to fuck? "What makes you think so?"

"The way his eyes follow you, wherever you go. How he both relaxes and grows more agitated when he's near you. The look on his face when you left."

Her breath hitched, pressure growing behind her face.

Ashley had turned around in the front passenger seat to look at her, and even Ben glanced in the rearview mirror.

"Anything I need to know?"

She rolled her eyes. Her brother-in-law sort of sucked at interpersonal relations. "Nope," she said with finality.

Subject closed.

She and Cody weren't right for each other. She'd known that from the moment she met him. They may be powerfully attracted to each other, but all they knew how to do was fight.

She closed her eyes and passed a hand over her face.

She just had to see him one more time and then she could walk away. Start her new life. Without him. And without her CJ Steele house.

Pain twisted in her heart, dragged down and gutted her. All her excitement for her new life without Jeremy had fled. Only emptiness remained.

Still, she had a short-term plan. Cody didn't know it, but she'd taken the cash Ben had transferred to him for the drop to Rabago. She had it in the duffel at her feet. She wasn't going to keep him involved any longer. She planned to find Jeremy and bring him to the meet-up. If they both showed up with the money, Rabago would have to let them walk away, clear of any obligation. If she didn't bring Jeremy, there was a good chance he'd end up dead. She owed him this much after he'd saved her life.

She fiddled with her phone in her lap, scheduling the Uber to take her to Jeremy's cousin's, then back to Colorado Springs that night. Yeah, it would cost a fortune, but it was worth it to be able to definitively put all this behind her.

She'd deal with the rest of her life tomorrow.

14

Cody prowled restlessly around his place while Mark unpacked weapons.

"Twenty members of my pack will be here in a few hours," Mark said. "I think that should be enough without you risking any from yours. I want everyone to stay in human form and use a gun. I can't explain away torn throats and claw slashes a second time."

He nodded absently, not asking when the first time had been. Everywhere he looked he saw signs of Melissa's stay. The rubber band she'd used to pull back her hair lay on the coffee table. She'd left the Chromebook he'd bought her in the kitchen, her clothes were stacked neatly folded on the dryer.

"I'll be in the garage if you need me," he mumbled, needing to be alone.

Dammit. He'd acted like an idiot. Had he really

accused her of being a gold-digger? That wasn't her, and he knew it. This was a woman who cared deeply about a piss-poor teen with blue hair, and about an abused shifter family she'd just met. A woman who said she'd never forgive his father for throwing him out. A woman who worried for her good-for-nothing ex-boyfriend who had endangered her life.

Why had he kept his identity as CJ Steele a secret from her?

The truth may be as simple as the fact he loved hearing her wax on about him. Did that mean she didn't care about him, the person? That she only cared about some ideal she'd created in her mind about who CJ Steele was?

Maybe.

Maybe not. She loved his work. And he was the man who'd created that work. Could she come to love him? Her body certainly responded to his touch. And the times when she'd let her guard down—which admittedly, he hadn't made easy— things had been easy between them. So easy, it might have scared the hell out of him. He'd never felt so close to a female, especially not one he'd just met. Especially not a human. *Part* human.

Part shifter.

But every time they got close, he had to shove her away. He'd been scornful, closed off, and a downright jackass on several occasions. Now that she had her sister and Stone back, she wouldn't need him. He'd have no excuse to be near her, to keep her close to him.

He should have marked her!

But no, that wouldn't change things for her. He'd still be in the same boat—needing a female who may not ever want to see him again.

If only he'd shown even a smidgen of charm. Of chivalry. If only he'd made more of an effort to get to know her, or to show her more of himself. Instead he'd been prickly and defensive.

Each minute that passed made him grow more agitated, as his true mate drew farther from him.

His fingers worked mindlessly, tinkering with the Ducati. Cleaning and greasing the same parts over and over again.

Minutes turned into hours. His mind fogged into a haze of self-abasement, alternating with the steely determination to win Melissa's affection at all cost as soon as Rabago had been taken care of.

The Denver pack began to arrive and he went inside to listen to Mark assigning roles and weapons.

His phone rang and he looked at the screen. "It's Stone," he told Mark and swiped the screen to answer. "What's up?"

"Melissa's gone." Ben's terse words send a sheet of ice over his skin.

"Where?" he croaked.

"I don't know. Ashley thinks she's headed back to the Springs for some reason. Be on the lookout."

She was going to the meet. The thought struck him with the surety of truth.

"Hang on a minute."

That duffel bag she'd left with—what had been in it? He'd seen all the things he'd bought her still lying around his place. He strode quickly to the closet where he'd stowed the cash and flung it open. The bag stood empty.

Fuck.

"She took the money. She's planning on going to the drop herself."

Ben swore loudly.

"I'll take care of it." He hung up before Ben could answer. There was nothing more to be said. Melissa would be walking into a death trap without enough shifter blood to save her from a bullet hole. He had to get there and head her off before she got killed. "Let's move," he barked, though he had no authority over Ben's pack.

He shoved a gun in the waistband of his jeans and jogged out to his truck, gunning it before the rest of the pack had finished filing outside. He tore off toward the meet location—the only place he could think to find her.

Mark's original plan had been to get his pack in stealthily, without being seen. Maybe he'd still play that angle. All Cody knew was that he had to get there before Melissa did. With his foot pressed flat to the accelerator, he screeched to the road that led to the abandoned lot Rabago had designated for the meeting. He hid his truck behind a hedge out on the road, not wanting to call attention to his arrival.

Hearing the crunch of tires, he shrank back into the shadows. The blue Range Rover that had been parked in front of Melissa's house that first night turned down the drive and he dived into a nearby ditch to hide. Two more cars followed it down the drive.

He fought the desire to shift to protect himself and his female and jogged along the ditch that led toward the lot.

The white Toyota pickup truck that had also been in front of Melissa's house was parked there, along with the blue Range Rover and other cars. Was the pickup Melissa's vehicle? He hadn't pictured her as the sort of girl who drove a pickup, but then, he'd misjudged her in at least a half-dozen ways, hadn't he?

The lot appeared to be a construction project that had never been finished. The concrete foundation and shell stood ghost-like against the dusky sky. He palmed his gun and moved quietly, skirting around behind the building.

Deep male voices echoed off the walls, distorting the sound and making it harder for him to track their location. They appeared to be dividing up, circling around.

"Hello?"

His heart stopped. It was Melissa's tight voice, calling out.

"We're here. We have the money. Jeremy recovered it for you." Her voice wavered on the lie.

"Yeah, I got it back from the guys who robbed you."

Who the fuck was that? Jeremy?

He ground his molars, wanting to kill the motherfucker. Had Melissa's intent been to make sure Jeremy came out of his mess clean? Was that why she'd risked her life to come here today? That bastard did not deserve her loyalty.

"Get down on your knees, hands behind your head," Rabago shouted.

Cody still couldn't see anyone, but it didn't sound like they were in the same area. He crept along a concrete wall and peered around a pillar. Melissa and Jeremy were on their knees, fingers clasped behind their heads. The duffel bag of money lay in front of them.

Shit.

This was bad. Rabago would shoot them both the second he verified the money was there and there was nothing Cody could do—not with Melissa so vulnerable.

He scented shifters all around—they must be moving in quietly.

Rabago and four men stepped into the area from all directions, surrounding Melissa and Jeremy, guns trained on their heads.

"Check it out." Rabago jerked his head toward the money.

One of his guys darted forward, running on bent knees, keeping his head ducked until he reached the bag. He grabbed it and dragged it back before looking inside. "Yeah, looks like it's all here."

Fuck.

Melissa's nostrils flared and she turned her head in his direction, as if she scented him. But that was impossible.

Rabago saw her head turn and whipped his gun around to aim in Cody's direction, firing.

"Melissa, get down," he shouted and jumped out, firing at Rabago and missing when the guy jumped behind a pillar. The crack of guns shooting from all directions echoed off the walls, deafening him.

Melissa and Jeremy dropped to the floor. The man with the money had been shot, and Jeremy crept toward the bag on his belly.

Cody bolted for Melissa, taking two bullets to the chest.

"*No!*" She lunged for him, horror streaking her features.

Her scream and the bullet wounds almost forced the change upon him, but he had to stay in human form if he wanted to help her. He tackled her back down to the floor and laid on her, keeping his head down.

"No," she sobbed. "Oh, God, no. Cody—"

"Hush, baby. Don't move."

She choked on her sob, stifling it in surprise. The silly female must have thought he was dying.

Jeremy almost took a bullet to the head—it struck the ground beside him.

Cody fired at Jeremy's shooter—Rabago. He got him right in the center of the forehead. He could thank his father for the ten years of target practice and hunting in his childhood.

The explosions of gunfire subsided and shifters ran through the area, looking as organized as trained militia.

Sirens sounded in the distance and Mark pulled out his phone. "Disappear, all but you three," he ordered, pointing at Jeremy, Cody, and Melissa.

Cody eased his weight off his female and helped her to her feet. "Are you all right, baby? Are you hurt?"

She shook her head, her lips forming into speech but no sound coming out. "Y-you're… shot? Okay. Right? Bleeding."

Poor baby. He pulled her against his side, holding her tight with one arm as he kept his gun loosely held with his free hand. "I'm fine. Unless it's a bullet to the head, shifters bounce right back." He kissed her hair. Her reaction to his bullet wounds had been forever imprinted in his mind.

She loved him.

Jeremy attempted to crawl to his feet, but Mark pointed his gun at him. "You stay on the fucking floor. Face down, hands behind your head."

Jeremy complied. The sirens grew louder.

"This is going to be a cluster fuck. Try to let me do the talking, all right?" Mark muttered. "Drop your gun, Steele."

He dropped the gun and wrapped both arms around Melissa. Her body trembled against his. "Shh. It's okay. It's over now. Everything's going to be fine," he murmured against her hair.

She shivered against him and pressed her body closer.

"I've got you, baby. I'm not letting go."

Not now. Not ever. Not for anything.

Mark Ruhl somehow managed to allow her and Cody to walk away after giving their statements, without having to go into the police station. Jeremy was not so lucky. But hey, he was alive. Beyond that, it wasn't her problem.

Cody held her snugly against her side the entire time, and now walked her to her truck. He opened the passenger door for her, though, and held out his hand for the keys.

Another time she might have argued. Right now, she could hardly form sentences, and the sight of Cody's blood-drenched clothing kept reminding her of the horror of the moment when she thought he'd been killed.

She should have known he was all right. Should have remembered from Ashley's story of Ben getting shot when she'd been blackmailed, but all she knew in the moment was white dread. Terrifying, heart-stopping fear that Cody had been murdered. Because of her. And in the shock of the moment, her greatest regret had been that he would die not knowing what he meant to her.

She climbed in the truck and sat, numbly waiting as Cody started it up and drove back into town. She didn't register their direction, or anything around her. Her ears still rang from the gunfire and the images of death flashed in front of her eyes in gruesome repetition.

"Cody…" Her voice cracked. She had to try to tell him—to make amends for the things she'd said. "I never thought you were… just a construction worker." Her tongue felt too big in her mouth. Pressure built behind her eyes and nose. "I'm sorry—"

"Hush, baby. I know."

"No, please… I want you to know something."

He turned to look at her, his face weary, eyes haunted. "What, baby?"

"I was bluffing," she whispered. "When I said it was just sex. Every time I pushed you away. You were too much my type and I was afraid of making another mistake, but I never thought you were beneath me."

Cody parked the truck and reached over to squeeze her fingers. She looked out the window, not recognizing the place. They were in the Old North End neighborhood, but not on his street. A huge Victorian brick house stood on a recently landscaped lot. The house had a worn look. Some of the siding trim had rotted in places, and it desperately needed a new roof and several coats of paint.

"Where are we?"

Cody didn't answer, but he walked around and opened her door for her, offering a hand to help her out. He tucked her back against his side and walked her to the door, pulling out his keys and fitting one into the lock.

"Is this one of your houses?"

"Yeah." He led her inside.

Her realtor's instincts kicked in, a blessed diversion from the shock of the scene they'd just left behind. She made mental notes about what would need to be done to make the place livable and how much it would deduct from the selling price. But no, if Cody owned this place, he would fix it up himself. Which meant he'd probably list this place for at least eight hundred thousand dollars. Way, way out of her range.

"It's not finished yet—obviously. I'm just getting started. But this is the house I thought you might like. It's the reason I didn't accept your offer on the other one."

She felt like her brain just couldn't get in gear. "I don't understand."

Cody released her, stepping back to rub his forehead. "It's bigger, see. Something we could grow into."

"*We?*"

Misery seeped into the lines on Cody's face. "Or you can have the other one, if you like it better. Or my place." His shoulders sagged. "You can have any house you want. Melissa—"

Tears pooled in her eyes. She drew a shaky breath, but didn't speak, wanting to be sure she understood what Cody was saying.

He lurched forward and caught both her hands. "Please don't cry. I need you, baby." He spun her and wrapped both his arms around her from behind. "This house, princess," he whispered, his breath feathering across her ear. "I'll make it perfect for you. For us, if you'll have me. There's room enough for pups, here. Lots of them if you want."

Something fluttered in her chest. The hope she'd been afraid to let herself feel. She laughed through the tears streaking her face. "I do want lots of them. At least three."

Cody stilled, then turned her slowly in his arms to face him. "Yeah?"

She nodded.

"With me?"

She cocked her head to the side. "Well, I was thinking I might live in your house but invite Jeremy—"

The inhuman growl from his throat made her

shriek as he plowed her against the wall and covered her mouth with his own, swallowing her laughter. His tongue lashed into her mouth as he yanked her knees up to his waist, pressing his bulging cock against her sex.

"That's not funny," he growled. He shoved two fingers in her mouth while his hips ground against her.

She sucked his fingers, heat flooding her core.

"Don't you ever say that name to me again." He yanked at the waistband of her jeans.

"Wait," she cried, afraid he'd rip them right off her body. "I'll take them off."

His eyes had turned pale blue. "I'm going to fuck that name right out of your consciousness. Understand?"

She almost orgasmed right there, just from his possessive threat. Her fingers fumbled on the button of her jeans and she shoved them down her hips.

He removed his fingers from her mouth and glowered. "Now, Melissa." Were his canines longer?

She ought to be afraid. He definitely might hurt her. Except she didn't care. She wanted him to claim her, own her, demand every last bit of her. With a couple of hops on one leg, she managed to untangle herself from the jeans and panties.

Before she'd even stood, Cody had her pinned back against the wall, shirt up to her neck, bra down. His lips clamped around one nipple and he sucked hard, teeth scraping across her sensitive flesh.

She screamed.

"You're my mate, Melissa. I need to claim you. I'm sorry, I don't know why I kept fighting it."

"I'm sorry, too. I wanted you to claim me but I was trying to protect myself from getting hurt."

He yanked open his jeans to free his cock. "I can't stop now," he grated and shoved into her without warning.

She shuddered, clenching around him. He snapped his hips and thrust again and again, while she continued to climax.

"Who do you belong to?" He roared it this time. "Say it."

"You! Cody Steele. Only you."

His teeth had definitely grown longer. She must've looked frightened, because he covered her eyes with his hand. "Don't look," he panted. "Don't move. Oh, God, please don't move." He sounded like he was in pain. Her pelvis banged against the wall behind her with bruising force as he fucked her hard and fast. "I can't stop," he moaned. "I don't want to hurt you, baby."

With her vision obscured, her need became even more intense. She pounded her fist on his rock-hard shoulder. "Do it," she yelled.

He shoved in deep. A sharp pain sliced into her shoulder, front and back.

She screamed.

His body shuddered and jerked, then gradually relaxed. The teeth came out and he licked the wound he'd inflicted, laving away the pain.

Her internal muscles still fluttered around his cock, but she, too, had relaxed, and a terrific sense of well-being filled her. She remembered Ashley saying the serum coating his teeth—the serum that had just marked her forever as his—produced a drug-like effect to ease her pain.

She sank into the wall, her muscles going limp.

"Baby…" Cody eased his hand from her eyes. "Oh, God, you're crying."

She shook her head. "No, I'm not."

But Cody thumbed tears away from her face.

"I'm sorry. Are you hurt? I mean, of course you're hurt. Fuck." He pulled out of her and shifted to scoop under her knees. "It's okay, baby. You're going to be all right." The anxiety on his face as he peered at her made her heart twist.

He cursed.

"Cody," she mumbled, wanting to soothe him. "I'm okay."

"Can you stand? Just for a second, so I can get your clothes back on?"

He dressed her, then swung her back up in his arms and carried her out to his truck. Although it was completely insane, and she tried to tell him so, Cody insisted on driving with her cradled on his lap, her back leaning against the door, feet spilling into the passenger side. Fortunately, it was less than a mile to his house.

He carried her into his house and onto his bed, where he sat with her nestled in his arms, dropping kisses on the top of her head as she drifted off to sleep, floating on a euphoria of love and peace.

CODY BALANCED the hot coffee and bag of breakfast sandwiches and muffins in one hand to unlock the door. The sound of the shower running made him smile. His mate was up.

Yes, *mate.*

The concept still stunned him on a minute by minute basis. He'd spent the entire night holding Melissa, watching her wounds close and start to heal, painfully slowly compared to a shifter, but still far faster than they would on a human.

Ben and Ashley had shown up at his door not long after they'd returned, but he'd refused to let them in. He'd been covered in his own blood and hers, and Ashley had been terrified, but Stone guessed at what had happened.

"You marked her," he'd said, nostrils flaring.

He half-expected Stone to challenge him, and his inner wolf growled, willing to fight to the death for her. But once he'd assured them she was all right, just sleeping off the serum and healing, they left.

The shower turned off. He set the coffee and goodies on the dresser and waited for her to emerge.

She came out with a towel wrapped under her armpits, her pale skin flushed from the water. The smile she flashed him dazzled.

He stepped over to her and moved her hair from her shoulder, examining her wounds for the millionth time, then kissing each one. "How are you, baby?"

"I feel wonderful, actually." She beamed up at him. She did, in fact, radiate good health and well-being. Her skin glowed, her eyes were bright, smile so full of joy, he wanted to be sure he never wiped it from her face again. "How are you?"

He'd showered and changed but hadn't slept—his worry over her had kept him up all night. "I'm fine—see." He grinned and pulled up his shirt to show her the bullet wounds had completely healed.

She reached out to brush her fingertips over his abs, sending a shudder of the deepest recognition through his being.

Mate.

He gripped the edges of her towel and pulled her up against his body. Her damp heat permeated his clothes, made his skin itch to be in direct contact. "We do have a score to settle before we can move forward."

Her eyes dilated, nipples stiffened against his ribs. "I was hoping you'd say that." Her voice was husky.

He slid his hand under the back of her hair and stroked her nape. Her arousal filled the room. He opened the corners of her towel wide, then let it drop, drinking in the sight of her. Now that he'd marked her, the itchiness was gone, but incinerating desire still flamed bright.

He kicked his shoes off and crawled up on the bed, settling with his back against the headboard and patting his knees.

She crawled over to him, her breasts bouncing with the movement, hair falling over her shoulders like a curtain. With a tug, he pulled her over his lap and popped each cheek with a loud smack.

She squirmed, hands flying back to cover her ass.

"Uh uh." He caught her wrists and pinned them against the small of her back with one hand, and delivered a few spanks with the other. "You don't get to cover."

"Ow," she cried. "Mercy!"

He laughed and rubbed her ass again. "I admit I am inclined to show you mercy. In fact, I'm prepared to worship between your legs for hours on end today."

She moaned and parted her legs.

His fingers slid between them, delving into her sweet nectar and rubbing it over her clit.

She raised her ass higher and parted her legs more.

"Baby, what happens after you've been punished?"

"My reward," she gasped immediately, as if she'd been waiting for it with great anticipation.

He chuckled and continued to rub between her legs. Her juices leaked from her exposed pussy, coating his fingers. His own desire took over and he rolled her onto her back and fell down over her, pinning her wrists above her head as he kissed and bit down her neck to suck the stiff peak of her nipple.

She wrapped her legs around his waist and pulled his hips against her core. "Take me," she breathed. "I need you now."

The beast roared to life within him. He tore off his shirt and shoved down his jeans, impaling her with his cock.

Her eyes flew wide, mouth opened, but only a strangled gasp came out.

"Is this what you need, baby?"

"Yes," she moaned.

He rocked into her again, shoving deep, stretching her wide. "I'm not wearing a condom, do you know why?"

"Why?" she gasped.

"Because I've claimed you, princess. And I'm going to put a pup in that sweet little belly of yours before the month is through."

He didn't even know where those words came from. He'd never thought about having pups, except in the very distant future. But mating Melissa had changed everything. The idea of starting a family with her seemed the only right thing in the world. Besides keeping her in his bed and making that smile stay on her face, forever.

"You're nuts," she laughed.

He leaned on his fists and pounded into her. "Is it okay? I'll pull out if you want me to," he managed to say.

"No!" she shrieked. "I'm so close."

"Come for me, princess."

She climaxed, her internal walls squeezing his cock, milking it. With a roar, he came, too, still fucking her deep and hard, thighs shaking with the pleasure of release.

He held himself up on his forearms and nipped her neck, kissing and sucking down to her shoulder. Still buried inside her, he stroked her hair back from her face.

"We can live in the house you put an offer on while I finish the big one," he said. He had a list of important items to discuss with her and didn't want to wait another minute.

The eye visible to him crinkled as she smiled. "What about this place? What will you use for a workshop?"

He kissed her temple and eased out of her. "This could still be my workshop. And my man cave when you get sick of me and kick me out."

She laughed. "No way. You don't get a man cave. Why don't we just stay here?"

"Because you hate this place."

She rolled over to face him and nestled right up into his arms. "I don't hate it. I wouldn't mind redecorating, though."

He kissed her nose. "Anything you want, baby."

She raked her fingernails through the hair on his chest. "I want to be your real estate agent."

"Yeah. I want that, too." It had been on his list of things to settle between them.

Her gaze flew to his. "You do?"

"Are you kidding? You think I'd let anyone else show my houses? Or help me buy them, for that matter? I didn't even know there was such a thing as the right buyer for a house until I met you. I'm not settling for anything less again."

She beamed at him.

He leaned his forehead against hers. "Are you really all in with me? No regrets?"

"Not yet." She flashed an impish smile. "I am a little nervous, though," she croaked a moment later.

"About what?" He wanted to slay every dragon she had.

"Everything. I'm afraid you'll change your mind. Or end up being an asshole, or a drug addict or pimp or something."

"We both already know I'm an asshole, so there's no solving that. But a mated wolf doesn't change his mind. Once you're marked, you're mine forever, baby, and I'll never grow tired of you. That's the way it works."

She looped her arms around his neck and kissed him. "Promise?"

"Alpha's promise." He kissed her back. "Do you really want kids?"

"Yep. Definitely."

"Right away?"

"Didn't you promise I'd be pregnant in a month?"

He grinned and pushed her onto her back, kissing her hard. "I'm sure as hell going to try, baby. Morning, noon, and night."

The End

For a special bonus scene featuring Cody and

Melissa's attendance at the shifter games in Estes Park, **click here.**

WANT MORE? THE ALPHA'S PROTECTION

The Alpha's Protection

His wolf wants to mark me. I can't let it happen.

On the run with my kids, the last thing I expect is to find my true mate.

He's magnificent--a shifter enforcer and a human lawman.

A true protector. He wants to shield us from danger. Take care of us.

He wants to claim me and make it forever.

But I can't let him. Not when it could cost him his life.

NOTE: This book was originally published as part of the USA Today Bestselling anthology, Daddy's Demands.

WANT MORE? THE ALPHA'S PROTECTION

READ NOW —>

tion, Theirs to Protect, Owned by the Marine, Theirs to Punish, The Alpha's Punishment, Disobedience at the Dressmaker's and *Her Billionaire Boss*. In addition to the free stories, you will also get special pricing, exclusive previews and news of new releases.

Shifter Ops

Alpha's Moon

Alpha's Vow

Alpha's Revenge

Alpha's Fire

Alpha's Rescue

Alpha's Command

Werewolves of Wall Street

Big Bad Boss: Midnight

Big Bad Boss: Moon Mad

Alpha Doms Series

The Alpha's Hunger

The Alpha's Promise

The Alpha's Punishment

The Alpha's Protection (Dirty Daddies)

Two Marks Series

Untamed

Tempted

Desired

Enticed

Wolf Ranch Series

Rough

Wild

Feral

Savage

Fierce

Ruthless

Contemporary

Chicago Sin

Den of Sins

Rooted in Sin

Made Men Series

Don't Tease Me

Don't Tempt Me

Don't Make Me

Chicago Bratva

"Prelude" in Black Light: Roulette War

The Director

The Fixer

"Owned" in Black Light: Roulette Rematch

The Enforcer

The Soldier

The Hacker

The Bookie

The Cleaner

The Player

The Gatekeeper

Alpha Mountain

Hero

Rebel

Warrior

Vegas Underground Mafia Romance

King of Diamonds

Mafia Daddy

Jack of Spades

Ace of Hearts

Joker's Wild

His Queen of Clubs

Dead Man's Hand

Wild Card

Daddy Rules Series

Fire Daddy

Hollywood Daddy

Stepbrother Daddy

Master Me Series

Her Royal Master

Her Russian Master

Her Marine Master

Yes, Doctor

Double Doms Series

Theirs to Punish

Theirs to Protect

Holiday Feel-Good

Scoring with Santa

Saved

Other Contemporary

Black Light: Valentine Roulette

Black Light: Roulette Redux

Black Light: Celebrity Roulette

Black Light: Roulette War

Black Light: Roulette Rematch

Punishing Portia (written as Darling Adams)

The Professor's Girl

Safe in his Arms

Sci-Fi

Zandian Masters Series

His Human Slave

His Human Prisoner

Training His Human

His Human Rebel

His Human Vessel

His Mate and Master

Zandian Pet

Their Zandian Mate

His Human Possession

Zandian Brides

Night of the Zandians

Bought by the Zandians

Mastered by the Zandians

Zandian Lights

Kept by the Zandian

Claimed by the Zandian

Stolen by the Zandian

Rescued by the Zandian

Other Sci-Fi

The Hand of Vengeance

Her Alien Masters

www.ingramcontent.com/pod-product-compliance
Lightning Source LLC
Chambersburg PA
CBHW070629100726
47907CB00007B/1910